# ROCKY MOUNTAIN VENOM

## BROTHERHOOD PROTECTORS COLORADO
### BOOK ELEVEN

## ELLE JAMES

TWISTED PAGE INC

# ROCKY MOUNTAIN VENOM

## BROTHERHOOD PROTECTORS COLORADO
### #11

*New York Times* & *USA Today*
Bestselling Author

**ELLE JAMES**

*Dedicated to my assistants Nora and Michelle for helping me get my books "seen". Thank you for all you do to keep me on track. You're awesome!*
*Elle James*

# AUTHOR'S NOTE

Enjoy other military books by Elle James

### *Brotherhood Protectors Colorado*
SEAL Salvation (#1)
Rocky Mountain Rescue (#2)
Ranger Redemption (#3)
Tactical Takeover (#4)
Colorado Conspiracy (#5)
Rocky Mountain Madness (#6)
Free Fall (#7)
Colorado Cold Case (#8)
Fool's Folly (#9)
Colorado Free Rein (#10)
Rocky Mountain Venom (#11)

Visit ellejames.com for more titles and release dates
Join her newsletter at
https://ellejames.com/contact/

# PROLOGUE

*2020 Late Spring, Helmand Province, Afghanistan*

"Venom, SITREP," Rico, Venom's "eyes on the ground," spoke softly into his ear.

Stars lit the sky overhead, casting light and shadows over the town.

From his perch atop an abandoned building with its entire west side reduced to rubble by shelling, Venom adjusted the sights on his .338 Lapua Magnum, high-end military sniper rifle. He set the crosshairs on the building Military Intelligence had identified as the one containing the Taliban leader they'd been after for the past two months in Afghanistan.

He could clearly see the entrance, the guards leaning against the walls on either side, their chins touching their chests, half, if not fully, asleep while standing at their posts.

"Nothing moving," Venom reported. "No sign of our bogey."

"Give it time. The sun will be up soon," Rico assured him.

The hardest part of being a sniper was waiting. A good sniper had to have the patience to wait for the best shot, the instinct to know it when he saw it and the skill to place the bullet exactly where he intended.

Venom drew a deep breath and let it out slowly, his finger caressing but not depressing the trigger.

This was the closest they'd come to finding Mullah Ghani, one of the cruelest leaders among the Taliban terrorists. The man was responsible for the beheadings of nine US Army soldiers, seven men and two females, from a supply convoy. They'd all been stripped, dragged through the streets and stood in front of a crowd. Then, one by one, they'd been executed by decapitation using a large machete.

Venom's teeth ground together. He'd seen the video downloaded from the Al Jazeera news site. He hoped to hell the families of those soldiers never had to witness that same video. He couldn't bleach the images from his memory. They replayed like a horror movie in his mind when he was awake and in his dreams.

Army Military Intelligence hadn't spared his

SEAL team from that display of brutality. The viewing had accomplished the goal.

Venom was out for blood, along with the rest of the team. They'd surrounded the small town in the dark and waited for sunrise. With too many women and children co-located with Ghani, they were to wait until the man left the building and pick him off with a well-placed shot.

That was Venom's job. As the number one sniper on the team, he didn't miss his target even at distances of up to, and sometimes exceeding, twenty-three hundred yards.

One by one, the stars disappeared as the gray light of pre-dawn washed over the heavens. That dusky, early-morning haze that wasn't light or dark made a person squint into the gloom, trying to make out shapes previously outlined by starlight.

Venom stared into his scope. The guards still stood at their posts, but now they appeared as shadowy blobs in their black garb.

As the murkiness lifted with the rising sun, Venom's view cleared. Despite being awake for over thirty-six hours, he was alert and ready to complete his mission. They had their orders. Ghani was their target. If he was there, they were to take him out. He was not to leave that village alive.

As the sun edged up over the horizon, doors opened in nearby stone and mud homes. Men, women and children emerged into the streets and alleys, going about their daily routines, unaware of the SEALs crouching in the shadows or, in Venom's case, lurking on the roof of one of the war-damaged buildings.

Venom had his exit plan in place. The other members of his team were counting on him to get the job done. They were closer to the target but well hidden. If the unthinkable happened and Venom missed, they'd move in and take out Ghani.

It would be more dangerous and far messier than a clean shot from a sniper's rifle. One bullet and done.

All his attention focused on the door to the building and keeping calm, cool and collected. Excitement was dangerous, making his pulse quicken, his heart race and his breathing unstable. He couldn't afford to let his body spin out of control. Deliberate breathing, steady hands and complete concentration guaranteed success.

For a brief moment, he leaned up, moving his eye away from his scope. He stared down the length of the Lapua's long barrel to the building in the distance. A woman wearing a black burka and carrying a basket passed by the two men standing guard.

They straightened away from the wall they'd been leaning on all night and stretched their arms.

A boy followed behind the woman, wearing white pants and a white shirt, kicking a soccer ball.

The woman turned and must have said something to the boy because he scurried to catch up to her. In his haste, he kicked the ball a little too hard. It hit the woman in the back of her legs and bounced sideways, rolling to a stop in front of one of the guards.

The guard bent and picked up the ball. Instead of throwing it to the boy, he threw it to the other guard.

Venom frowned.

The boy stopped following the woman and stared at the two guards.

Too far away to hear the boy or the guards, Venom could only guess what they were saying. Clearly, the guards were teasing the boy, probably threatening to keep the ball.

"The door's opening," Rico murmured into Venom's ear.

Venom repositioned himself with his eye behind the scope that was trained on that door.

Two men dressed like the other two sentries emerged, carrying AK-47s.

The guard with the ball quickly set it on the ground against the building. He straightened as the two men who'd come out of the building took positions beside the door.

The men who'd been there all night talked with the newcomers for a few minutes and then disappeared around the side of the building.

The boy's mother must have called out to the child. He turned and raced to follow her.

Moments later, a dark SUV rounded a corner and stopped before the guards. The two men who'd been up all night got out and stood beside the vehicle, weapons at the ready.

The building's door opened again. Three men emerged. Two men in black trousers and carrying rifles flanked a man with a long gray beard, wearing a full-length black robe and turban.

Venom, his finger resting against the trigger, focused on the man with the white beard. He'd studied the images intelligence had provided. This was their target.

Ghani.

One of the bodyguards moved between Ghani and the business end of the Lapua.

Venom waited patiently, though he knew he had to take the shot before Ghani stepped into the vehicle.

The bodyguard shifted, giving Venom the break he needed.

He drew in a breath, held it and gently squeezed the trigger.

As the bullet left the barrel, a flurry of motion flashed through his scope.

Too late to stop the bullet, Venom held his breath and watched through the scope.

Ghani turned as a small white figure dashed past him.

The bullet struck Ghani. The man jerked, his hands flew up, and he swayed. Then he crumpled to the ground and lay still.

That's when Venom saw what was behind Ghani.

His heart arrested in his chest.

"Fuck." Rico's curse sounded like the sharp report of rifle fire in Venom's ear.

The sound of a woman's scream carried from that distant street all the way up to where Venom remained frozen in his position on the bombed-out building.

The burka-clad female burst into view, threw her basket to the ground and flung herself to the ground next to what looked like a small pile of white rags, stained in crimson.

*No, no, no.*

Venom's heart squeezed hard in his chest at the visceral sound of grief echoing against the walls of the buildings.

The bullet meant for Ghani had hit the target, passed through the man and hit the little boy, racing by to retrieve his ball.

Venom had taken out his share of terrorists, but never…never a child.

They'd call it collateral damage.

Fuck that shit. A child wasn't a statistic. A second ago, that little boy had been a living, breathing human with a mother who loved him and all his life ahead of him. Now…

Venom's stomach roiled. It was all he could do to keep from puking his guts out.

"Time to move to the extraction point," Rico said. "Venom, we'll pass your position in less than one mike. Be ready."

Despite the flurry of Taliban soldiers swarming out of the building, Venom couldn't drag his gaze away from the woman holding her child against her breast, rocking back and forth, her cries gut-wrenching in her despair.

"Venom!" Rico called out. "You copy?"

Venom squeezed his eyes shut, blocking the image of the boy and his mother. "Roger," he said into his headset.

"Be ready, damn you." Rico breathed hard into his mic as he ran through the streets, headed toward Venom. "We don't have time to pull your ass down from your perch."

"I'll be ready." Venom opened his eyes, grabbed his weapon and made his way down what was left of a staircase to ground-level. He'd just picked his way through the rubble when Rico, Lopez, Janek, Wallis and Miller rounded a corner, heading in his direction.

"Go!" Rico yelled.

Gunfire behind them made Miller and Wallis spin and return fire, covering for the others to make their way out of the town to the ridge east of town where the helicopter would land long enough for them to jump aboard.

Though his rifle was suitable for long-distance sniper shots, it was too heavy and unwieldy for close combat. Venom ran for the extraction point, keeping pace with Janek and Lopez. Rico and Lopez stopped to provide cover for Miller and Wallis as they leapfrogged past. Venom would have taken his turn providing cover had he carried the M4A1 rifle or a submachine gun. The best he could do was to get himself to the extraction point.

As he stared out at the ridge, his gut clenched. The helicopter wasn't there and wasn't anywhere in sight. He didn't let that slow him down. He ran faster. If he could make the ridge, he could turn and pick off the enemy combatants.

Venom made the ridge yards ahead of the others, spun and dropped to the ground. In seconds, he had the Lapua positioned and ready.

As his team raced toward him, he fired over the heads of his team members at the Taliban fighters, his aim as accurate as ever. There were more terrorists than the small team of SEALs. No matter how many Venom took out, there would be more than he could effectively stop. The Lapua was designed for sniper fire, and the magazine only held five rounds at a time, meaning Venom had to stop to reload often, wasting valuable time.

Janek, Lopez and Miller made it to the ridge.

Wallis caught a bullet, stumbled and fell.

Rico, as only Rico could do, turned his machine gun on the advancing Taliban soldiers and yelled his signature warrior cry, unloading the remaining bullets in his magazine.

He dropped to the ground beside Wallis, expelled the empty magazine and shoved another into the gun.

"Rico, get your ass back here!" Venom cried.

Rico came up with Wallis, one arm around his waist, firing and running backward as he did.

Wallis limped but fired his rifle as they made their way up the hill.

The rest of the team laid down a repressive stream of fire, but it wouldn't hold for long. They were quickly running out of ammunition.

"Where's our Uber?" Rico called out as he reached the top of the ridge and crossed over the other side with Wallis clinging to him.

Venom didn't have time to answer; the Taliban were closing in. He pulled out his Sig Sauer P-226 handgun and fired until he ran out of ammo.

"Get down," Janek cried out. "Uber's almost here."

As the thump of rotors echoed off the hills, the Navy SEALs ducked behind the ridge.

The Black Hawk Helicopter swooped in, 50-caliber machine guns raining the fires of hell down on the advancing terrorists.

Some fired up at the helicopter, then turned and ran toward the village to take cover behind buildings.

The chopper lowered over the ridge, continuing to fire.

Venom leaped to his feet and ran to help Rico. With one man on either side of the injured SEAL, they got him into the chopper, then climbed aboard.

Once the team was safely on board, the bird lifted off the ground.

As they rose into the sky, Venom stared down at

the town growing smaller by the second. He couldn't see the little boy, but he saw him in his mind, kicking the ball and then lying as still as death, his white tunic drenched in blood.

Rico clamped a hand on Venom's shoulder.

"Don't," Venom bit out.

Rico frowned. "Don't what?"

"Don't say it?" He shook his head. "He wasn't collateral damage. He was a little boy. I should've seen him coming."

Rico squeezed his shoulder and let go. "Shit happens."

*Yeah, shit happens*, Venom thought. Unfortunately, it happened to people who never asked for it, by people like him dishing it out.

# CHAPTER 1

"Sofia and I need to use the restroom." Clutching her five-year-old daughter's hand, Maria Elena Garcia stopped in the middle of the shopping mall and turned to face the man following three steps behind her.

She forced a smile for her bodyguard, praying her poker face was sufficient to convince the man that going to the restroom was her only plan. Thankfully, the sunglasses she'd worn to hide her black eye hid the fear surely visible in her eyes.

Raul's eyes narrowed briefly before he tipped his chin toward a hallway in the mall. "I'll wait outside the door," he grunted, his Hispanic accent heavy, having grown up in the border town of Juarez, across the river from El Paso, Texas.

Maria's boyfriend, hopefully, soon-to-be ex-boyfriend, Diego Valdez, insisted that every time she crossed the border from Mexico back into El Paso, she go escorted by him or with one of the men he called bodyguards, like Raul. Only they weren't bodyguards. They were more like prison guards.

Diego insisted they were there to protect her and their daughter, which wasn't entirely incorrect. He was, after all, the son of one of the most notorious cartel leaders, Xavier Valdez, better known as el Martillo...the Hammer. Another fact Maria hadn't been aware of when she'd started dating the handsome young man with a swagger and confidence that made women fall all over themselves to be with him.

Fresh out of a four-year commitment to the US Army, Maria had been flattered that Diego had chosen her over the other girls with whom she'd been celebrating her separation from active duty. She'd purchased a sexy dress, painted her nails and worn her long dark hair down around her shoulders, feeling more feminine than she had for a long time. She was starting a new chapter, free of military regulations, uniforms and taking orders.

Diego had told her she outshined the stars that night. His attention and compliments had made her feel special and ready for whatever would come next in her life. He'd set out to woo her, courting her until he'd convinced her to move in with him.

Had she known what a relationship with Diego Valdez would mean to her freedom, Maria would have run the other way seven years ago when they'd first been introduced by a mutual friend at that Cinco de Mayo celebration in El Paso.

They'd been together for seven years. Not because Maria had been happy with Diego.

Maria led Sofia down the short hallway to the Ladies' restroom.

Raul followed closely behind her.

Taking a deep breath, she pushed through the swinging door, noting Raul's position as he leaned against the wall, preparing to wait for Maria and Sofia to complete their business.

As soon as the door swung closed, Maria hurried around the corner to the rows of stalls and headed straight for the far wall.

"I don't have to go potty," Sofia said.

"Okay, *mi querida*," Maria said. As she reached the wall, she stared up at the window six feet off the ground and then looked around the room for something to climb up on.

That window might be the only chance she and Sofia had to make their escape. And only if they moved quickly.

After checking that the stalls were empty, she knelt beside her daughter and pulled off her sunglasses.

Maria cupped her child's cheek with one hand and pointed upward with the other. "Sofia, do you see that window up there?" she whispered.

Sofia's gaze rose, and she nodded and then returned her glance to her mother.

"We're going to go through that window and leave the mall," Maria continued.

Sofia's eyes widened. "Mr. Raul will be mad."

"It's okay. We're going far away from him."

"And Diego?" Sofia had never referred to her biological father as Daddy. Diego had insisted she call him Diego, claiming it was to protect her if no one believed she was his kid. Maria knew the truth. Diego didn't want the responsibility of being a father.

"We're not going back to his house." Maria stared into her daughter's eyes.

Sofia's brow dipped low, and her lips pressed together. She reached out and touched Maria's bruised eye. "He won't hurt us anymore?"

Maria swallowed hard to dislodge the lump in her throat. "That's right. He's never going to hurt us again."

Sofia glanced up at the window and, in a very grownup voice, said, "We better hurry."

Maria gave her a watery smile and straightened. "That's right." As quietly as she could, she dragged a metal trash receptacle across the floor and turned it upside down, spilling crumpled paper towels across the tile. Then she climbed up onto the metal container and tried to unlock the window. When it wouldn't open, she removed her jacket and one of her shoes. Pressing the jacket against the glass, she held it there and slammed her shoe against the jacket. The fabric muffled the sound, but the glass didn't break.

Maria figured they only had five minutes before Raul got antsy and checked on what was taking them so long. Since the shoe wasn't working, she used the next hardest thing she had available.

Ducking her head, she rammed it into the jacket-covered glass. It shattered, spewing shards outward.

For a moment, she held her breath, afraid the noise, no matter how muffled, would alert Raul.

When the bodyguard didn't burst into the bathroom, Maria let the air escape her lungs and went to work. She wrapped her arm with the jacket, quickly clearing the jagged remains from the frame, then laid the garment over the frame and peered out at the Texas sunshine. Below the window was hardpacked dirt, not concrete.

Her daughter reached up.

Maria bent and lifted her up into her arms. "Go through the window, and I'll lower you to the ground. Then I'll climb through right behind you."

Sofia didn't cry, cling or appear frightened. Instead, she nodded, leaned out of her mother's arms and clambered up onto the window frame.

Maria took her hands and lowered her to the ground.

The squeak of the restroom's swinging door made Maria stiffen. She shot a glance over her shoulder.

A woman had entered the bathroom and stood staring wide-eyed at Maria.

Maria pressed a finger to her lips. "Please, don't say anything. That man outside the door is holding us hostage. This is the only way we can escape."

The woman pressed her hand to her mouth, her

eyes widening even more. "I have a cell phone. Do you want me to call the police?" She dug into her purse and held up the cell phone.

"No," Maria answered quickly. "My boyfriend has connections with dirty cops. I have to get as far away from here as I can."

The woman nodded solemnly. "Here, take the phone and hurry."

"No," Maria held up her hand. "I can't take your cell phone."

The woman held it up. "Take it. You need to call someone to help. It's hard enough to leave an abusive relationship. If you have family or friends, call them."

Maria took the cell phone. "Thank you."

Another squeak of the swinging door made Maria's heart flutter. She pulled herself through the small window and dropped hands-first onto the ground, rolling into a somersault before pushing to her feet.

Sofia huddled in the shadows against the side of the building. When Maria reached for her, she wrapped her arms around her neck. "Hurry," she said.

Maria ran. Carrying Sofia slowed her down a little, but her determination to get her daughter somewhere safe made her push harder. As she emerged into the parking lot, she made a beeline for the black SUV they'd arrived in. She'd seen one of the bodyguards reach beneath the driver's door frame on a number of occasions to retrieve a magnetic box containing a spare key to the vehicle.

If the key box wasn't there, she and Sofia would have to continue on foot. They wouldn't get far enough fast enough to escape Diego's web of informants and minions.

The key had to be there.

Maria felt along the bottom of the chassis, running her hand the length of the two doors.

Nothing.

She dropped to the ground, lay on her back and searched beneath the SUV.

There.

The small, magnetic box she was looking for clung to the undercarriage.

She yanked it loose, rolled to her feet, pulled the key from the box and tossed the box aside. Thankfully, Diego had taken the newer SUV with the automatic door locks and key fobs. The vehicle he'd assigned for her use was an older model with keys to unlock the doors and start the engine.

She quickly unlocked the vehicle and opened the back door for Sofia to climb in.

Without being told, her daughter buckled her seatbelt.

Maria slipped into the driver's seat, slid the key into the ignition and started the engine. As she backed out of the parking space, she looked all around. It wouldn't be long before Raul realized she'd fled. He'd notify Diego immediately. That didn't give her much time to get out of El Paso.

Her first attempt to escape had been when she'd found out she was pregnant with Sofia.

Diego had caught up with her before she'd left the city limits of El Paso. He'd taken her to his father's compound in Mexico, south of Juarez, and had kept her locked in a room until close to her due date. He'd brought her back over the border to deliver the baby in a US hospital.

Since then, he'd taken her back to Mexico and kept her locked in his father's compound. As time passed, he'd loosened his grip on her life only enough to allow her to cross the border into the US to shop for clothing and items for Sofia. And only with him or with one of his trusted henchmen. Never alone.

Maria hadn't tried to escape again. Not with a small child. That other time, she hadn't made it far on her own. With an infant or toddler, escape would be even more difficult.

She'd suffered Diego's abuse, taking the punches and broken ribs. Accepting it as part of the life she'd let herself become a part of.

Until a week ago.

Diego had come to their rooms in the compound after a night out drinking with his friends.

She'd been reading a book to Sofia when Diego slammed through the door.

He'd cursed at her for reading to her in English instead of Spanish.

Maria had immediately stood and urged her daughter to go to her room.

Diego had demanded she let Sofia stay and let her papa read to her in Spanish.

Maria stood between Diego and Sofia. "You're drunk," she'd stated. "Let her go to her room."

His face had flushed with anger as he'd stomped across the room and slapped Maria so hard across her face she'd crashed to the floor.

Horrified, Sofia had rushed at her father and pounded her little fists into his legs, which only made Diego angrier.

He backhanded Sofia, sending her flying across the room. She lay flat on her back for several seconds before she moved,

Maria scrambled to her feet and rushed to her daughter, throwing her body over Sofia's small, crumpled form. "If you have to hit someone, pick on someone your size," she'd spat out.

So, he had. He yanked her to her feet and punched her in the gut and in the face several times before he flung her away from him. "Take the brat and get out of my sight."

Her eye swelling shut and aching in every part of her body, Maria had gathered a silently sobbing Sofia and left Diego in the sitting area of their quarters. She'd slept in Sofia's room that night and every night through the following week.

During that time, she'd formulated a plan to escape. She'd put up with Diego's abuse because she'd known he wouldn't let her go. Even if he did allow her to go, he'd never let her take Sofia.

After he'd knocked their daughter across the room, Maria knew she had to fight to keep her daughter safe. As long as they were under Diego's control, Sofia wouldn't be safe.

When Diego slept, Maria slipped into his room and stole bills from his money clip. A few dollars at a time, praying he wouldn't notice.

Maria didn't have a credit card, bank account or cell phone of her own. To get far away, she'd have to have transportation. She'd often watched Diego's minions reach beneath the older SUV for the key when he'd wanted the vehicle moved after someone else had taken the keys into the compound.

She'd played nice to Diego, pretending all was well with her and Sofia for the week following the incident. Then she'd asked for a trip to the mall in El Paso for clothes and shoes for Sofia, claiming she'd outgrown her existing wardrobe.

Diego frowned. "Tell Raul what you need, and he can get it."

Maria shook her head. "She needs to try on clothes and shoes to ensure they fit."

Diego's frown had deepened, but eventually, he'd agreed. Whether it was out of a general desire to provide for his daughter or guilt for having hit her, Maria hadn't cared. She just wanted to cross back into the US and find a way to get Sofia away from Diego.

Diego leaned out into the hallway and yelled for Raul.

When the man appeared, Diego pulled some large bills out of his money clip and handed them to Raul. "I'll be heading over the border as well."

He turned to Maria. "The mall and back. No side trips."

Maria had nodded, keeping her chin down and not making eye contact. She'd wanted Diego to think she was easily commanded and compliant to his wishes. After all, hadn't she been just that for the past five and a half years?

She shifted into drive, feeling a little awkward behind the wheel after over five years of relying on others to drive her where she needed to go. At the same time, her back stiffened.

She could not...would not get caught. Each time she stopped at a traffic light, her pulse quickened, and her gaze swept 360 degrees around her, expecting Diego's men to show up at any moment.

Remembering the cell phone the stranger had given her, she pulled the device out of her pocket and stared down at it for a moment. The woman had told her to call someone...family...a friend—anyone who could help.

Her parents were gone, having died in an auto accident shortly after she'd hooked up with Diego. They'd never gotten to know their only grandchild. Sofia would have loved Maria's mother and father. And they would have been so proud of the little girl with the soulful brown eyes and the ability to smile no matter what life threw her way. In this case, no matter what punches her father threw her way.

Maria had cousins east of El Paso in San Antonio. She shook her head. Diego knew about them. Family members would be the first place he would look, assuming she got out of El Paso without being captured.

If she hoped to keep her whereabouts secret, she couldn't go to family. Diego had cut her off from the friends she'd had when they'd met. Most had been Army friends who'd stayed on active duty and had transferred from Fort Bliss to other areas of the country or around the world.

Then she remembered a friend from when she'd been deployed to Afghanistan. A friend who'd suffered more than Maria at the hands of another service member. She'd been buried alive and left to die.

"JoJo," she whispered.

If anyone would know what she was going through, JoJo would. And JoJo had been one tough cookie, ready to stand up for the underdog and kick ass if the situation called for it.

The last Maria had heard from her before Diego had cut off all her communications, JoJo had been medically retired and returned home.

Before her abduction and almost death, the spitfire mechanic had talked nonstop about her home in the Colorado Rockies outside an old mining town. Maria wracked her brain for the name and anything else that might help her find her old friend.

She'd said it was on the other side of some mountains from Fort Carson. Where was that?

At another traffic signal, she searched the phone's screen for a map application. Once she found one, she pulled up Fort Carson, Colorado, and zoomed out on the map. The light changed, and she had to move with the flow of traffic.

As much as she wanted to drive straight out of town, she knew she had to have a place to go and a route to get there. One that didn't take her onto the interstate or major highways in the area.

Rather than drive aimlessly, she checked her rearview mirror for the hundredth time, then pulled into an alley and parked behind a large trash container.

She twisted in her seat to glance back at her daughter. "Hey, baby, are you all right back there?"

Sofia nodded. "Should we keep going so Raul won't find us?"

She smiled at her daughter. "We will. I just need to know where we're going." Returning her attention to the cell phone map, she searched the area around Fort Carson and Colorado Springs, her gaze tracing roads leading through mountain passes until she came to a town called Fool's Gold.

"That's it." JoJo had talked about being taken in by her friend's Marine Corps father after her parents had died unexpectantly. The retired Marine and his daughter had run a dude ranch. How many dude ranches could there be in Fool's Gold?

She searched the internet for dude ranches near Fool's Gold, Colorado, finally striking her own gold with Lost Valley Ranch. The search even provided a phone number.

She pressed the call button and held the phone to her ear, praying JoJo had landed there after leaving the Army and that her delay wouldn't cost them everything.

After the second ring, a gruff voice answered, "Lost Valley Ranch, Gunny speaking."

Tears filled Maria's eyes. Gunny was the crusty old Marine JoJo had spoken of with such warm affection. She swallowed hard to dislodge a lump in her throat. "Gunny, is JoJo there?" She held her breath, waiting for him to say she wasn't. Or worse, that he didn't know who she was talking about.

After a long pause, she heard him shout as if at a distance, "Jojo! Telephone!"

Maria released the breath she'd held. Tears slipped down her cheeks.

"Give her a minute; she's coming up from the barn," Gunny said, and then silence reigned for an eternity that might only have been a minute.

"This is JoJo," her friend's familiar voice came across the line like a blast from a past that had been an entirely different lifetime.

"JoJo." Maria's voice cracked as more tears fell and sobs threatened to choke her.

"Yes, this is JoJo. Who's this?"

A quick glance in the rearview mirror reminded her that she didn't have time to fall apart. Her daughter needed her to be strong. Connecting to her old Army friend brought back that confidence and strength she'd had while in uniform—before Diego had beat her down mentally and physically. "You might not remember me, but we were deployed together in Afghanistan. This is Maria Elena." She gave a weak laugh. "You knew me as Garcia."

"Garcia? The chick from El Paso who could eat jalapeños like nobody's business?"

Maria laughed, her heart warming at the shared memory of a jalapeño-eating contest they'd had one night after she'd received a jar in the mail from her parents. "That's me."

"So, Garcia, how's life treating you? I heard you left the Army. That's been a while back. Where are you? What are you doing now?"

She hated calling out of the blue and laying it on heavy with a friend she hadn't seen since deployment a hundred years ago, but desperate times...

"I need help," Maria said.

"What kind of help?" JoJo's voice grew serious.

"I've left an abusive relationship and need a place to hide."

"Can you go to the police and get a restraining order?" JoJo asked.

Maria snorted. "My ex owns half the police force in El Paso and has informants all over the city."

"Are you in El Paso now?" JoJo's voice was urgent. "Do you need me to come down there and get you? Your ex doesn't own me."

For the first time in years, Maria felt a glimmer of hope swell in her chest. "I took one of his vehicles and a little cash. I think I can get far enough away before I run out of gas and cash. I need a place to go."

"You'll come here," JoJo said. "Are you sure you don't want me to meet you halfway? I can be on the road in ten minutes."

"No. I think I can make it if I get going soon. I hate to impose. I mean, we haven't talked in years—"

"Time doesn't change who we are," JoJo said softly. "You're my friend. If I can help, I will. Come to Lost Valley Ranch; it's just outside of Fool's Gold, Colorado. I'll make sure you're safe."

"JoJo, you should also know I won't be alone." Her gaze went to the rearview mirror where her daughter sat quietly, her brow furrowed as she stared out the window, probably looking for Raul. "I'm bringing my daughter, Sofia."

At her name, Sofia met her gaze in the mirror.

"Good," JoJo said. "We'll make sure she's safe as well."

"One other thing you should know…" This was the part she hated admitting to anyone because it made her feel stupid and naïve for having gotten into the situation in the first place. "My ex is the son of a drug cartel kingpin. He won't let us go easily. Taking us in will put you in danger."

"Shit, Garcia. Even more reason for you to get your ass up here in a hurry. I really think we should head your way. If he's got half the assets you think he does, you might not make it."

"All the more reason for me to get moving," Maria said.

"Are you using a phone he can trace?" JoJo asked.

"No," Maria said.

"Has he tagged the vehicle you're in with a tracking device?"

"That I can't tell you."

"Put your phone on speaker."

Unfamiliar with the phone, Maria fumbled to do just that. When she succeeded, she said, "On speaker."

"Open the contacts and add me." She waited for Maria to open the app and gave her cell phone number.

Maria keyed it into her contact information.

"Now, share your location with me. That way, I can track your progress."

Again, she searched through the device until she found how to share her location.

"Interstate 25 will get you here faster," JoJo said.

"He'll have people out on interstates 25 and 10, expecting me to take the fastest route out of town."

"Okay, then take Highway 54 to Santa Rosa. It's about halfway. We'll meet you there and bring you the rest of the way in one of our vehicles. Most likely, he has the one you're in tagged with a tracker. Most importantly, you need to get out of town."

Maria entered Santa Rosa as her destination on the cell phone's map application and hit Go. "I'm on my way."

"If I don't come, I'll send someone even better skilled at protection to make certain you and your daughter are safe. I'll let you know who to expect before you get to Santa Rosa."

"On my way as we speak," Maria said, pulling out of the alley onto the street. She hadn't considered that the vehicle she was in might be rigged with a tracking device. If it was, no matter where she went, Diego could track her. Her stomach roiled at the thought. She needed the SUV to get away faster, and she didn't have the money to rent a car. Besides, a rental agency would require a credit card, which she didn't have, and a driver's license that had long ago expired.

JoJo had been right to insist on sending someone to meet her halfway. Hell, she hoped she'd make it halfway before Diego caught up with her.

"Garcia," JoJo cut into her thoughts. "You still with me?"

"I'm here," she responded.

"You're doing the right thing."

"That's all I needed to hear," Maria whispered. Even if she had to ditch the SUV, she would get to Fool's Gold. "I'll see you soon."

# CHAPTER 2

"I'VE BEEN with Brotherhood Protectors for over a week now." Venom paced the length of the basement conference room at the Lost Valley Lodge. "I've shoveled horse manure in the barn, helped sling burgers at Gunny's Watering Hole and strung fence along the property boundary. You sure you don't have an assignment for me? I don't mind doing all those things, but I feel like I'm not earning my pay."

"Sorry about that. We've hit a bit of a lull. Trust me, it won't last long, and we'll have more work than we have men to handle. That's where you'll come in." Jake Cogburn handed him a 9-millimeter Glock and grabbed one for himself. "In the meantime, let's go some target practice."

The cool metal in his hands felt familiar, comfortable and alien all at the same time. "I'm still not convinced I'll be the right man for this job."

Jake limped toward him and clapped his free hand

on Venom's shoulder. "Oh, you will be. We only hire the best of the best. You have to be ready to take the downtime along with the insane missions."

"I've been out of the Navy for too long. I'm rusty."

"All the more reason to do some target practice." Jake glanced down at the handgun. "Though this wasn't your weapon of choice. You want to take one of the Lapuas out for a ride?"

Venom stiffened, heat rushing through his body at the mention of the last weapon he'd fired in the Navy. The one that had killed Ghani and the little boy who'd only wanted to retrieve his soccer ball. "No."

Jake stared into Venom's gaze. "I read your file. You haven't touched a Lapua since your last mission to Afghanistan."

Venom's jaw tightened. What else did Jake know? The mission had been Top Secret. Only those with a need to know would have knowledge of the target or the resulting collateral fucking damage.

His fingers curled into fists as the image of the boy clad in white clutched to his mother's chest flooded his memory. "That's right," he said. "And?"

Jake held his gaze a moment longer and then shrugged. "Nothing. It's just that you chalked up quite a record of hits with that rifle. I'd have thought you'd stay with what worked for you."

"I separated from the Navy not long after that mission," he stated, his tone flat. "As a janitor, I had little need to maintain my skills on that weapon."

Yeah, the only job he'd found upon leaving the Navy had been that of a high school janitor. The fact he was a veteran was the only thing going for him. Who needed an expert sniper in the civilian world?

Hank Patterson, the founder of the Brotherhood Protectors, had asked him to join his team of security specialists not long after he'd announced that he was leaving the Navy after fourteen years of service. He'd turned him down. Why would he trade one violent career for another?

Six more years and Venom could have retired with a pension and benefits. Instead, he'd chucked all he'd worked so hard to achieve to start over. And for what?

To wash graffiti off walls and scrub toilets for ungrateful, moody teenagers who'd never gone hungry or had to worry about walking home through a minefield.

They didn't know how lucky they were to live in a country with relatively little violence. Where they could drive their cars to football games and go out on dates. The only thing they had to worry about was what to wear and which fast food joint they'd meet their friends at that evening.

After two painful years of quietly cleaning floors, windows and bathrooms, he'd been ready to shoot himself.

That's when Hank had sent Jake Cogburn out to recruit him away from his prized position on the high school's bottom rung. This time when asked if he wanted to come to work as a Brotherhood Protector, he'd been ready to leave behind his toilet brush, the teens and California for the Rocky Mountains of Colorado and something more rewarding than cleaning up after a food fight in the cafeteria.

Why was he complaining now?

Because he needed to work. To have a mission. To make a difference.

A door opened above, and footsteps clattered down the stairs. "Jake!"

JoJo, the ranch mechanic, raced down the stairs, a frown denting her forehead. "Jake." When she spotted him, she hurried across to stand in front of him, her breathing ragged. "I have a job for the Brotherhood Protectors."

The petite woman with her long dark hair pulled back in a ponytail and grease smudged across her cheek continued without waiting for Jake's response. "A friend of mine from my Army days just called. She's on her way here, running from an abusive ex. We need to send someone to meet her halfway. I'm afraid her ex will catch up with her before she can get all the way here."

Jake laid his hands on her shoulders. "Slow down and start over. Who's coming here?"

"Garcia. We served together in Afghanistan. She's on her way here from El Paso in a vehicle belonging to her ex. I'll bet money he has a tracking device on it. The bastard belongs to a drug cartel. He probably tracks all their vehicles. In which case, she might not make it all the way here before they catch up with her. But if you send someone down now, he can meet her halfway, ditch her car and lose the tracker."

"How far out of El Paso is she?"

JoJo grimaced. "She just left."

Jake frowned. "I could have someone drive down there, but what if she runs into trouble sooner than halfway?" He pulled his cell phone out of his pocket. "Is she coming up Interstate 25?"

"No, she didn't want to take the obvious routes out of the city. She's heading north on Highway 54. I told her we'd meet her in Santa Rosa."

"We might be able to do better than that," Jake said.

"Only if you break every speed record and avoid law enforcement," JoJo said. "At posted limits, it's a little over five hours to Santa Rosa,"

"If you drive." Jake grinned and punched a number on his cell phone. "Hey, Tayo, are you at the Springs airport?" He paused, his brow creasing. "I see. Is your buddy who flies your jumps available? Yeah. Get back with me ASAP. I might need him to fly one of our guys to a drop in New Mexico." He ended the call.

"Are you talking about a parachute drop?" Venom asked, his blood pushing through his veins, a familiar rush of adrenaline getting his heart pumping faster.

"How long has it been since you've jumped?" Jake asked.

"Years," Venom said. "But I had over five hundred jumps."

"And more important, you had five hundred successful landings based on the fact you're standing here today." Jake's grin faded, and then he shook his head. "No, I can't have you jump if you haven't done it in a while and with unfamiliar equipment."

"What about Tayo?" JoJo asked.

"He's in Denver with Kayla." Jake glanced down at his leg. "Like Venom, I haven't jumped in years, and I'm not sure how it would be with a prosthetic." He patted his artificial leg just below his knee.

Venom had been shocked the man had lost his leg and was now the head of the Colorado Division of Brotherhood Protectors.

"Guess we'll have to send someone by land." Jake turned to Venom. "The rest of the guys are assigned or away. That leaves you and me. If you think you're ready, I'll send you."

"I'm ready," Venom answered almost before Jake finished his sentence. "And if a plane is available, we might be able to find a small airport for it to land between here and El Paso."

"True." Jake limped over to the array of monitors mounted against one wall and dropped into a chair. He brought up the internet and an image of a map depicting the route between El Paso and Santa Rosa, New Mexico.

"I'm not nearly as fast as someone else," he muttered and brought up another screen on a different monitor. Moments later, he had a video call going with Hank Patterson's computer guru, Axel Svenson, otherwise known as Swede, another former Navy SEAL Venom had heard about, but never crossed paths with.

"Got a situation I need your skills to help with," Jake said.

Swede nodded. "Shoot."

Jake quickly explained. "I need to know the airports where I can land a small plane between El Paso and Santa Rosa, that might also have access to a rental car."

JoJo came to stand behind Jake. "Why not bring her back in the airplane?"

Jake and Swede both shook their heads. "If we bring her back to Colorado Springs, her ex, if he knows anything about planes, could trace the plane there," Swede said.

JoJo frowned. "We don't want him anywhere close."

"If she doesn't park the car at the airport, he might not know she took off in a plane," Venom pointed out.

"So, we need an FBO with a loaner vehicle if we don't find one with a rental car." Swede's fingers clicked across a keyboard out of sight of his camera.

"Just to be safe, we can pick up Garcia, take her to the waiting plane and transport her to a larger airport where someone can meet her that her ex doesn't know." Venom poked his thumb at his chest.

"Like me. I can rent a car and bring her the rest of the way to Fool's Gold."

Jake grinned. "And you don't have to jump. Hell, I could do that mission." He held up his hand. "Don't worry. This will be your assignment. What you need to do now is to get on the road to the general aviation terminal at the Colorado Springs Airport. If the plane isn't available, you'll be driving to Santa Rosa."

Jake's cell phone rang. He answered, "Cog here." As he listened, his lips curved in a smile and he gave Venom a thumbs-up. "My man, Venom, will be there in forty minutes."

"I'm sending you a list of airports along Highway 54 with their phone numbers," Swede said. A nearby printer fired up and spit out a sheet. "Each of them has loaner cars. When you get close, call and let them know you're on your way in and need the loaner."

Jake handed the page to Venom. "The plane will be waiting at the FBO."

Venom spun and headed toward the stairs.

Jake's voice called out, "Hey, you might need this."

He turned in time to catch the shoulder holster Jake tossed his way.

"You might need that and some ammo for that Glock you have." Jake chuckled.

Venom hadn't realized he still had the weapon in his hand. He gathered two magazines of rounds, slipped the holster over his shoulders, snagged his leather jacket from the back of a chair and headed up the stairs.

"Wait." JoJo raced up behind him and grabbed his sleeve. "Take my phone. She shared her location with me so I could track her progress. You can also use it to contact her when you've determined a place to meet." She slid her cell phone into his breast pocket. "Please hurry. She sounded desperate. Also, I might not have mentioned it, but her ex is the son of a drug cartel kingpin out of Juarez."

Jake crossed the room. "Drug cartels have massive networks. We might need to send more people to do this job."

"Do you have anyone else available immediately?" Venom asked.

Jake spread his arms wide. "You're looking at him." He turned and gathered his Glock, ammo and a shoulder holster. To JoJo he said, "Let RJ know—"

"—you'll be late for dinner." JoJo nodded. "Just go. Take care of my friend and bring them back alive."

Venom assumed by JoJo's reference to *them* she meant Garcia and himself since he was the new Brotherhood Protector. Did she have such little faith in him that she thought he needed Jake to cover his six?

Frankly, Venom was glad Jake was going along. He wasn't sure of the rules of engagement in the civilian world. All he'd ever known was combat on foreign soil.

"I'll drive," Venom said.

"You're on." Jake followed him out to his truck.

As they drove into Fool's Gold and down the

winding road through the mountain pass into Colorado Springs, the men discussed their plan of attack. Jake compared the airport locations to the map on his cell phone. Where they landed would depend on how far Garcia had come by the time they intercepted her. Jake called the pilot and informed him that they were going to the airport in a town called Vaughn. Swede had marked it as the town where they'd most likely intercept Garcia. The pilot would file a flight plan and be ready to go when they arrived. After he ended the call to the pilot, he called the Vaughn airport and asked to have a rental car or a loaner ready for when they arrived.

Jake guided Venom through Colorado Springs traffic to the general aviation side. They parked and hurried through the facility and out onto the tarmac where a small twin-engine airplane waited.

They climbed aboard and made their way up to the cockpit where the pilot worked through his pre-flight checklist and contacted ground control to get clearance to taxi the active runway.

The pilot had invited Jake to sit in the co-pilot's seat.

As soon as Venom settled into the seat behind them, the cell phone in his breast pocket vibrated. He pulled it out and read the text.

Ten miles south of Alamogordo. So far, no tail.

Venom knew exactly where she was, having opened the tracking app as soon as he'd boarded the plane. He realized Garcia probably didn't know she wasn't talking to her friend JoJo. He didn't want to alarm her now by letting her know someone else had JoJo's phone. Instead, he responded,

Roger. Will contact you with meeting instructions as we get closer.

The pilot taxied to the designated runway. Soon, they were in position behind a 737 commercial airliner, next in line to take off.

After the 737 left the ground, their airplane lined up on the runway. Moments later, they were in the air, heading south.

Venom listened to Jake explain to the pilot that they were on their way to pick up a passenger and that they would have him fly them to the airport in Albuquerque. He didn't tell them any more than he had to. Not that he didn't trust the pilot, but they'd agreed the less the pilot knew the fewer questions he could answer should the cartel somehow connect any dots and trace Garcia to him.

The flight was uneventful. Based on where Garcia was, they'd arrive in Vaughn before she did, giving them time to locate a vehicle and find a meeting location away from the airport. Venom would text her that location, and they'd wait for her to arrive.

Though not as intense as moving through a Taliban-held town, the mission had Venom's blood coursing through his veins, making him feel more alive than he'd felt since he'd left the Navy.

Two hours in flight passed quickly. Other than the occasional contact with ATC and casual conversation between the pilot and Jake discussing the best places to go whitewater rafting, the trip proved uneventful and strangely relaxing. Had he driven the route, he wouldn't have made it to Santa Rosa before Garcia, and he'd have had to navigate a lot more traffic than what they'd encountered in the air.

As the pilot brought the plane down and rolled to a stop next to the FBO, the cell phone in Venom's hand pinged with an incoming text. They'd been out of cell phone reception at a higher altitude.

He glanced at a message that had been sent fifteen minutes earlier.

Thirty-five miles south of Vaughn, should make Santa Rosa in an hour.

Which meant she would be in Vaughn in fifteen or twenty minutes.

The pilot shut down the engines.

Venom released his seatbelt. "Our passenger will be in Vaughn in fifteen mikes," he said into his headset. Then he peeled the headset off and moved to the exit.

As soon as the propellers stopped spinning, Venom opened the door and dropped to the ground.

Jake eased out beside him as a man emerged from the building carrying a clipboard with rental documents and a pen. "Sign here, and she's all yours for the day."

After Jake scribbled his name on the bottom line, the man handed him the keys. He thanked the man and tossed the keys to Venom.

They drove through the gate leading out of the airport and into the town of Vaughn.

Jake had the map up on his cell phone. "There isn't much to this town. Pull into the back of the Travel Lodge parking lot. We'll make the switch there."

The Travel Lodge was the last major landmark before a Y in the road where Highway 54 turned left toward Santa Rosa and 285 went straight toward Roswell.

Venom drove to the back of the Travel Lodge. As he shifted into Park, the cell phone pinged with an incoming text.

Entering Vaughn. Dark SUV following me for the last ten miles. Now closing fast. Might be a tail.

"She's entering Vaughn with a possible tail," Venom said aloud as he quickly keyed,

Blow through Vaughn. Turn into Travel Lodge parking lot all the way to the back. Two men will be waiting for you. You can trust them.

He hit send and opened his car door. "She'll be coming in hot."

"If it is a tail," Jake said. "Get her into the car and hunker low. "I'll take her vehicle and drive it out of Vaughn and take the Y going south on Highway 285 toward Roswell. Once you're reasonably sure you're in the clear, head to the airport."

Venom nodded and jogged to the corner of the building where he had a view of the main road

Garcia would be turning off as she entered the hotel parking lot.

Based on the map, Vaughn wasn't very big with maybe a handful of houses, an RV park and a few convenience stores to service the travelers passing through.

Garcia would be there any moment now.

A dark SUV barely slowed as it skidded sideways into the parking lot and raced to the far end of the hotel.

As the vehicle slid to a stop, Venom was there, yanking open the driver's door.

A pretty, dark-haired woman wearing sunglasses jumped out. "They were right behind me until a truck pulled out in front of them. We don't have much time."

"I'm Venom." He nodded toward Jake. "That's Jake. JoJo sent us. Come with me." He grabbed her arm and started for the car as Jake climbed into the SUV.

"No! Wait!" Garcia jerked free of Venom's hold and turned back to the SUV. She yanked open the back door and reached in for something on the back seat.

On the other side of the heavily tinted windows, Venom couldn't see what she was getting until she emerged carrying a small, dark-haired child, wearing a white shirt and light blue shorts.

Venom's breath lodged in his lungs, and his heart

dropped to the pit of his belly. "No one said anything about a child," he whispered.

If Garcia heard his words, she didn't respond. She ducked around him and ran for the car with the doors standing wide open. She shoved the child into the back seat and dove in after her, pulling the door closed behind her.

"I've got this," Jake said as he pushed the back door shut and slid into the driver's seat. He slammed the shift into drive, punched the accelerator and rounded the back of the hotel. As planned, he drove around the other side of the building heading toward Roswell.

Venom's head spun with images of a small boy dressed in white with a large red stain spreading across his chest.

Moments after Jake passed on the highway, another dark SUV passed, picking up speed as they reached the edge of town. The trailing SUV raced up to the back of the one Jake was driving and rammed into the rear.

The attack forced Venom out of his daze and into the car.

He shot a glance at the woman hovering over the child hunkered low on the back seat. She had eased up to the window and stared out at the highway.

"Did that SUV just ram into the back of the one your friend is driving?" Garcia asked.

"Looks that way," Venom shifted into drive and

waited to see what would happen between the two SUVs.

Jake's vehicle shot forward, increasing the gap between it and the trailing vehicle. It sped up. Just before it reached Jake's vehicle, Jake suddenly slammed on the brakes.

The driver of the trailing SUV must have jerked the steering wheel at the last moment. It spun, clipping the right rear bumper of Jake's before it ran off the road and plowed through a fence into a field.

Jake's vehicle fish-tailed, straightened and then continued down the road toward Roswell.

They hadn't talked about how Jake would get back to Fool's Gold, but at that moment, Venom had to get Garcia and the child out of Vaughn.

He headed northeast on Highway 54, slowed at the turnoff to the airport and hesitated. If they flew out of the airport, the man who'd rented them the car would see the woman and child. Vaughn was a really small town. It wouldn't take long to question every inhabitant.

Venom laid his foot down on the accelerator and blew past the airport road.

Like it or not, he was stuck transporting Garcia the rest of the way to Fool's Gold, which made him responsible not only for her but for the child as well.

Try as he might, he couldn't erase the horrible feeling of déjà vu and a nagging echo from the back of his mind...

*Collateral damage.*

# CHAPTER 3

THE CAR MARIA found herself in had no tinting to hide the passengers in the back seat. So, she remained hunkered below the windows for several minutes.

"Are we being followed?" she finally asked.

The man driving shook his head. "Not yet."

Given the nature of the terrain, if they were being followed, Garcia figured the driver would know pretty quickly.

She sat up and looked out the back window.

The road was empty, and dry brown fields to either side stretched for miles.

"Which way are we headed?" she asked.

"North toward Santa Rosa," he said, his deep voice as smooth and warm as melted chocolate.

Maria shook her head. Where that thought had come from, she wasn't entirely sure. Probably from the exhaustion of stress and driving for miles through long boring stretches of road with no trees and few buildings. Since she'd left El Paso, she'd felt as if she'd stepped out into the open, exposed to anyone who happened to spot her. Maybe she would have been better off driving into the Davis Mountains and losing herself through curvy roads and canyons.

"I hope your friend is okay," she said softly.

"Jake will land on his feet." The man glanced up, his gaze meeting hers in the rearview mirror.

He had gray eyes, a welcome change from Diego's brown-black eyes that shot daggers of disdain at her for every little infraction he'd imagined she'd committed.

She studied the back of his sandy-blond head and the breadth of his shoulders beneath the leather jacket he wore.

"What did you say your name was?" she asked.

"People call me Venom," he answered.

Her lips twisted. "Is that a reflection of your personality, or did your mother not love you?"

Again, his gaze met hers in the mirrored reflection. "It's a nickname my team came up with that stuck."

"Your team? Military, football or some other sport?"

"Military," he said.

One-word responses, huh? Well, if that's how he wanted to play it, she'd keep asking. "Branch?"

"Navy."

"Special Ops?"

He nodded.

"SEAL?"

"Ding, ding, ding. Give the woman a prize."

She snorted. "You could have relayed all that in one short sentence and saved time."

"And missed out on a game of twenty questions?" He chuckled. "I think not."

"Then I have about ten more," she said, smirking at him in the mirror. "What's your given name? Something worse than Venom, like Cornelius or Sidney?"

"Worse than that. Vincent."

"Nothing wrong with Vincent," she said.

Sofia looked up at her from where she sat with her knees to her chin on the floorboard. "Mommy, can I sit on the seat?"

Maria reached for her daughter, helped her up on the seat beside her and buckled the seatbelt across her lap.

"Is Mr. Vincent taking us somewhere Diego can't find us?" Sofia asked in a whisper.

Maria put her arm around her daughter and held her close. "Yes, *hermosa chica*." She kissed the top of her head. "He's going to take us to my friend JoJo. She lives in the mountains."

Sofia's eyes widened. "Real mountains with snow on top?"

Maria smiled. "I don't know if they have snow on top in the summer."

"They do," her driver responded. "Most of it melts in the summer, but not all."

Sofia clapped her hands. "Can I play in the snow?"

"I don't know." Maria brushed the hair out of her daughter's face. "It might be on top of the mountains where we can't go."

Sofia's gaze went to their driver. "Will you take me up to the snow, Mr. Vincent? I've never seen snow, except on television or in picture books."

"We'll see when we get where we're going," Venom said.

"We'll see," Sofia echoed, her smile turning upside down. "That means no."

Maria's heart ached. Diego had always said *we'll see*, and it had meant it wouldn't happen. Sofia might be five years old, but she was an old soul who saw through lies.

"If we stay in the mountains long enough," Maria touched her daughter's cheek, "it will snow enough for you to make a snowman and throw snowballs."

"When will it snow?" her daughter asked.

"In a few months," Maria promised, wondering if they'd stay in Colorado long enough for Sofia to experience the chilly wonder of snow, something she'd never had the opportunity to touch, having lived in Mexico for most of her life. They'd had an ice storm, leaving the roads slick and treacherous, but it hadn't lasted long before it melted. Slip-sliding on ice wasn't nearly as magical as lying in the soft, fluffy stuff making snow angels.

"Mr. Vincent, will you show me how to build a snowman?" Sofia asked.

He opened his mouth and started to say, "We'll se —" He frowned into the mirror before changing his response to, "Yes. As soon as we find enough snow, I'll show you how to build a snowman."

Sofia clapped her hands. "I'm so glad we're going to the mountains. And I'm glad Mr. Vincent is going with us. I don't think he'll let Diego take us back to Mexico or hit us again."

Venom's gaze went to Maria.

She was glad her sunglasses hid the evidence of Diego's abuse. The last thing she wanted from her rescuer was pity. She'd made a terrible decision, falling for a drug dealer's son and then another by moving in with him, thinking she could change him and make him give up the cartel life. Those had been her decisions and ones she'd punished herself for over the past five years.

But Sofia had done no wrong and didn't deserve the life Diego had cursed her with. Maria wouldn't go back to Diego or the Valdez family even if her life depended on it.

She glanced back at the long stretch of road, still empty of other traffic. "How did you get here so quickly? I thought your trip should have taken longer."

"We came by plane and landed at the small airfield just outside Vaughn."

"Is that why you slowed as you drove away from the little town?"

He nodded. "Internal debate on flying versus driving."

"And driving won," she stated. "It would be faster to fly there."

"Your tail was too close and the town too small. It wouldn't take them long to discover a strange woman and her child if they climbed aboard a small aircraft. Once they knew that, they could trace that aircraft from Vaughn back to Colorado Springs."

"Bringing them too close for comfort," Maria concluded. She settled back in her seat. "So, we drive the rest of the way. Do you need me to navigate?"

His lips quirked. "I have GPS on my cell phone."

"I'll take that as a *no*." She pulled the seatbelt over her lap and secured the buckle.

Sofia leaned against her shoulder and looked up at her. "Don't worry, Mommy. We're going to be all right. Mr. Vincent will take care of us, won't you?" She turned her gaze to the gray eyes in the rearview mirror.

Venom's brow crinkled in a frown. For a long moment, he stared at the road ahead. Finally, his gaze met Maria's. "I'll do the best I can," he said, his voice gruff, as if heavy…with what?

Emotion?

The thought made Maria study those gray eyes. The man was a highly trained Navy SEAL. Even if he was no longer on active duty. What was it they said?

Once a SEAL, always a SEAL. They earned that right through their brutal BUD/S training, where only twenty-five to thirty percent made it all the way through.

If anyone could get them safely to Fool's Gold, Venom would be the one.

"How do you know JoJo?" she asked.

His lips twisted. "I don't know her well. But she works at the Lost Valley Ranch, where the security company I work for has a regional office."

Maria's brow dipped. "Security company?"

He nodded. "It's called Brotherhood Protectors."

"Could you clue me in without using the last of my twenty questions? I have a need to know who's providing protection for me and my daughter. And just so you know, I have nothing. No money. And what you see is what you get. We couldn't pack our bags before we left. Bottom line is, if this is going to cost me, I don't have a way to pay."

Venom's expression softened. "I'm new to the organization, but what I've learned so far is that it's the dreamchild of Navy SEAL Hank Patterson. He and his wife, Sadie McClain, set it up to help others when the police or government, including the military, can't or won't get involved. They'll take on missions regardless of a client's ability to pay."

Maria sighed. "Thank God. I hadn't thought beyond getting away. I'm completely at the mercy of a friend I haven't seen in years. She might not even have the capacity to help us for long, and I don't expect her to." She ran a hand through her hair. "I'll get a job as soon as I can. I might need to change my name so Diego can't find us." The more she thought through her escape, the more she realized she hadn't thought past getting away. The magnitude of what she had to do now threatened to overwhelm her.

Sofia rubbed her arm. "We're going to be all right. We have each other."

Maria glanced down at her daughter. Escape might prove to have been the easy part. Reimagining her life would be hard.

"You did the right thing," Venom said softly, echoing JoJo's sentiment.

Maria knew they were right. Without a doubt, getting Sofia away from Diego was all that mattered. "I know," she said. "Now, I have to figure out how to keep us safe. The Valdez family doesn't give up what they consider theirs. They'll keep looking for us."

"The Brotherhood Protectors will provide your protection," he assured her.

"For how long?" Maria shook her head. "They can't do it forever. We'll have to go into hiding or leave the country."

"Hank's got good people working for him. Smart people, who will help you figure out your next steps," Venom said. "For now, we'll focus on getting you to Fool's Gold."

"You're right. I can worry about what happens next then." After another glance over her shoulder to make sure they weren't being followed, she leaned her head back against the seat and closed her eyes. For the first time since their daring escape through the bathroom window, she let herself breathe and relax. The tension of the past several hours eased a little. Even though she couldn't sleep, she could conserve energy in case she needed it.

Her thoughts spun. Diego would be furious. However, one question had been answered. They'd known where to find her. Which meant the SUV had been equipped with a tracking device.

A cell phone chirped.

Maria's head came up, and she searched for the device the woman had given her in the bathroom.

"It's mine," Venom said, answering the call with, "Dude, you okay?" For a few seconds, he listened.

Maria could hear a male voice but couldn't make out the words.

"Good. As long as they didn't see you and can't identify the driver, you should be all right. Glad you caught a ride with the trucker and that he wasn't from anywhere around there... Makes sense." Venom shot a glance in the rearview mirror. "They're okay. Roger. I'll keep you informed. See you back at the ranch in six hours, give or take."

Venom ended the call and met her gaze in the mirror.

"Your friend get away?" Maria asked.

"He did." Venom's lips quirked. "After they slammed into his bumper and ran off the road, Jake was able to put distance between them. He drove another fifteen miles, ditched the SUV on a farm road and caught a ride with an eighteen-wheeler headed back to Vaughn."

Maria frowned. "What if they went back to town to ask questions?"

Venom grinned. "As the truck headed northwest, it passed the banged-up SUV heading toward the vehicle he'd ditched. He's going to ride with the truck all the way to Albuquerque and have the plane pick him up there. He'll be back in Colorado Springs before we are."

A weight lifted from Maria's shoulders. "Thank God. Had something bad happened to him, I would've felt like it was my fault."

"How would it have been your fault?"

"It should have been me in that SUV, not Jake." She looped her arm around her daughter's shoulders, feeling guilty that Jake had taken the brunt of the attack from Diego's men. At the same time, she was glad she and Sofia hadn't been in the vehicle when it had been rammed from behind. She couldn't have handled it as well as Jake had.

Venom shot a frown at her through the mirror. "You didn't provoke those men to attack that SUV."

"By running away from my ex, they would've considered that provocation enough," she pointed out.

"You did what you had to," he said.

Maria sighed. "I know. And I'd do it again. I just don't want others to suffer the fallout from my bad decisions. They're aiming for me. I don't want others to become collateral damage."

The car swerved off the road onto the shoulder before Venom straightened the wheel and brought it back between the lines.

Maria twisted to look behind her. "Did you see something?"

"Nothing behind us," he said, his jaw tight, his brow creased.

"What happened? Why did you swerve?" She asked.

"Rabbit," he bit out.

"Oh."

Sofia leaned forward, her eyes wide. "Did you hit it?"

"No," Venom said, his tone softer. "I missed it."

"Good." Sofia leaned back. "It might be a mama bunny with baby bunnies waiting for her to come home."

"Then she'll make it home," he said, his gaze on the road ahead.

Maria hadn't seen a rabbit on the road. Of course, she wasn't driving and might have missed it. Still... something about the way Venom blamed his sudden swerve on a rabbit didn't ring true. His body had stiffened, and his jaw was so tight a muscle twitched beneath his stubbled skin. Up until a couple of minutes ago, he'd glanced back often, making eye contact with her.

Now, it was as if he didn't want to meet her gaze. As if he was actually avoiding it.

What had caused him to shut down? Had she said something that had made him angry?

Maria thought back over what they'd been discussing before Venom had swerved onto the shoulder. They'd talked about the attack on the SUV. She'd admitted to feeling guilty that others might be hurt defending her.

Why would that make him angry?

There was so much she didn't know about this stranger who held her and her daughter's lives in his hands.

She hadn't come all this way to continue to be the doormat she'd been with Diego. "Did I say something that upset you?" she asked softly.

"No," he responded. A single short sound that didn't invite further questions.

Maria was undeterred. She'd kept her mouth shut for the past five years for fear of incurring Diego's wrath, often not knowing what would set him off. She'd be damned if she kept her mouth shut now. Better to piss him off by asking questions than to tiptoe through a landmine of careless words and set off explosions of rage.

She crossed her arms over her chest, "I said something; otherwise, you wouldn't have swerved or bit off our heads over questions expressing our concern."

If possible, his shoulders and jaw got even stiffer,

and his lips pursed into a tight line. "It was a damned rabbit," he insisted. "Nothing more and nothing less."

Maria pushed. "I was talking about how I felt guilty that Jake took the SUV and how I didn't want him to become collateral damage trying to protect me."

"Don't," Venom ground out between clenched teeth.

"Don't what?" Maria tipped her head, her eyebrows descending. "I'm confused. Do you take issue with me feeling guilty and not wanting others to become—"

Venom held up his hand. "Don't say that."

"Collateral damage?" Maria said it before she could stop herself.

Venom winced with what looked like anguish flashing in his eyes before he narrowed them and gave all his focus to the road ahead.

"Why the aversion to those words?" she asked.

He lifted his chin, and his nostrils flared. "No more questions."

"I'm just trying to understand," she said softly. "I don't want to say or do anything that offends or… causes you pain."

"Please," he whispered.

Sofia leaned forward and touched the man's arm, concern etched in the crease across her little forehead. "Mr. Vincent, are you sad?" Maria's daughter had a gift for feeling the pain in others.

For a long moment, Venom didn't respond.

Had he not heard Sofia's question? Or was he ignoring it?

Maria wanted to know the answer as much as her daughter. What had happened in his past to cause such a visceral reaction to two words?

Collateral damage.

The man was a Navy SEAL. Had his actions during a mission resulted in collateral damage?

"Sofia, we should let Mr. Vincent have some quiet time," she whispered.

Sofia nodded, the crease remaining between her eyebrows. She shifted her gaze to her mother's, tears filling her eyes, "I wish he wasn't so sad." She whispered so softly that Maria had to lean closer to hear her words.

Her heart clenched. She gathered Sofia into her arms and held her as silent tears slid down her cheeks.

The child had been through a lot that day and for the past five years. Even if Diego hadn't raised a hand to her for most of that, the way he'd treated Maria had to have left a mark on her empathetic daughter.

For a long time, Maria held her daughter, wishing she'd gotten her daughter out much sooner. She prayed Sofia didn't suffer the lasting effects of PTSD from her life with Diego.

She couldn't have a do-over of the years that had passed, but she could do better with Sofia's future.

If they made it to Fool's Gold, and if Diego didn't find them.

# CHAPTER 4

VENOM KICKED himself for snapping at Garcia and ignoring Sofia's innocent question, asking him if he was sad.

Hell, yes, he was sad. And angry and had been since that little soccer-kicking boy had died from the bullet that had come from his gun. Ever since that incident, he'd questioned his own belief in what he'd been doing as a Navy SEAL. Had he been fighting for a just cause? Were the people he'd targeted really that bad?

In most cases, yes. But not in the case of the little boy. He hadn't asked to be caught in the middle of a war. All he'd wanted was to play with his soccer ball and be a child.

The little girl in the back seat wasn't the boy back in Afghanistan, but her situation had some similarities.

Sofia hadn't asked to be abused by the son of a

cartel leader. Thankfully, her mother had been brave enough to make a run for freedom for both of them. After living in an abusive situation, knowing the family in charge wouldn't let her go without a fight, she'd had the courage and cleverness to find a way out. It had been hard enough to free herself, but she'd brought a small child with her.

He admired Garcia's spunk and determination to get her daughter away from the cartel and the man who'd abused them.

After a long silence, he calmed down and realized he'd reacted poorly. He glanced into the rearview mirror, ready to apologize for snapping at Garcia and her child. They'd been through enough. They didn't need a grumpy protector, making them miserable for the rest of the journey to Fool's Gold.

He opened his mouth to apologize, only to close it again.

Garcia's head had tipped back against the seat.

Because she wore dark sunglasses, Venom couldn't tell if she was awake or asleep. He assumed she was sleeping and shifted his glance to the little girl.

Sofia met his gaze with one of her own that seemed to look right through him.

God, he hoped he didn't fail this child. He tipped his head and whispered so as not to wake her mother, "I'm sorry I was rude."

"It's okay," Sofia said. "Words can't hurt you."

*But hands, sticks and bullets could,* he thought.

Was that a light purple bruise on the girl's cheek? He couldn't tell at that distance and through a reflection in the mirror. His fingers tightened around the steering wheel until his knuckles turned white.

How could a man hit a woman, much less a child?

"Sometimes words hurt you here," he said, touching his chest.

Sofia lifted her chin. "Mommy says, only if you let them."

"Still, I wasn't nice to you and your mother. I'm sorry. I won't be that way again."

"And I'm sorry for poking a sore spot," Garcia said without lifting her head. "You asked me to stop saying it." Her red lips twisted in a grimace. "I should've recognized how much it bothered you."

"I didn't mean to wake you," he said, returning his attention to the road.

Movement from the back seat made him look again.

Garcia had pushed her sunglasses up into her hair, exposing the dark bluish-purple bruise around her right eye.

The sight kicked Venom in the gut. "He did that to you?" he asked through clenched teeth.

She started to pull the glasses back down to cover her eyes, hesitated and pushed them back up. "I'm fine. No bones broken."

"He broke bones before?" he asked.

She turned away and stared out a side window. By not answering his question, she'd answered.

Venom wanted to turn the vehicle around, drive down to El Paso and pound the bastard into a bloody pulp. No man had the right to beat a woman.

"The past is behind us. I refuse to dwell in it like a pig in a slurry of mud." Her lips curled in half a smile. "Actually, a pig might enjoy a slurry of mud. I most certainly wouldn't." She leaned toward Sofia. "Would you, *mija*?"

"Ew." Sofia's nose wrinkled. "No."

"Then why don't we focus on the present and a future without mud?" She held out her hand to the girl. "Deal?"

The girl took her mother's hand and shook it. "Deal."

"If you could live anywhere you wanted, where would it be?" Garcia asked.

Venom expected the little girl to say in a castle like a princess.

Not Sofia.

She tilted her head to one side and tapped a finger to her chin. "I'd live in a little house in the mountains where there are tall trees, a stream to wade in and snow in the winter." She smiled at Venom in the mirror. "Mr. Vincent could come to visit, and we'd build a snowman. Then we'd build a snowwoman and little snow children to keep him company." She grinned. "Mr. Vincent, have you ever built a snow dog or snow cat?"

He chuckled. "Can't say that I have."

Sofia frowned. "How can they be a snow family

without a snow dog and a snow cat?" She shrugged. "We'll have enough snow to figure it out."

Garcia brushed a lock of hair off her daughter's forehead. "Yes, we will. And a house in the mountains sounds lovely."

"When we get our house in the mountains, can we have a real dog and a real cat?" Sofia looked up into her mother's eyes with a soulful expression that bored a hole straight through Venom's heart. How could a mother refuse her child anything when she looked at her like that?

"Hold onto that dream," Garcia said. "I'll have to work hard to get all of that." She gave an unsteady laugh. "It's been a while since I've had a job. But I'm smart and learn fast. I'll find something."

Sofia nodded, her expression solemn. "I'll work hard, too."

Garcia hugged her daughter. "You're a good girl, Sofia."

The dark-haired little girl shook her head. "Diego told me I was bad."

Her mother set her at arm's length and stared down at her. "He was wrong. You defended me when he was the one being bad."

"He kept hitting you," Sofia's eyes filled.

*Holy shit.* Venom's heart ached at the emotion choking Sofia's words and the tears sliding down her cheeks.

He fought the urge to pull to the side of the road and wrap her and her mother in his arms. He wanted to hold them, protect them and keep them safe. To take away their bad dreams and memories and fill their days with sunshine and walks beside a mountain stream.

What the hell was he thinking? He was in no condition to care for a woman and a child. He could barely take care of himself. What kind of emotional support could a man like him provide when he stayed awake at night, afraid to sleep? Afraid the same dream would come back to haunt him.

He shook his head. This mother and child needed someone with his head squarely on his shoulders. A man who would never raise his hand or voice in anger. One with a steady day job that didn't include scrubbing food off a cafeteria floor.

*You have a steady job with the Brotherhood Protectors,* he reminded himself. He lacked that part about having his head squarely on his shoulders. The psych counselor that worked at the VA hospital in Colorado Springs, what was her name?

Emma? Emily?

Whatever. She'd been at the Lost Valley Lodge with Cage Weaver, another one of the Brotherhood Protectors who worked under Jake.

While the others had discussed the pros and cons of four-wheelers versus side-by-sides, she'd cornered him about the circles beneath his eyes. "Having trouble sleeping at night?"

He'd nodded, looking for a way to excuse himself without appearing rude.

She'd nodded knowingly. "Bad dreams?"

Venom had shrugged, trying to get Jake's attention to motion him over. The man had been deep into a debate about small engines and had his back to Venom.

"How long have you had trouble with dreams and sleeping?" she'd persisted.

"I don't know," he'd lied. Venom knew damn well it had everything to do with that final shot that had killed two when it had been meant for one.

She'd crossed her arms over her chest and positioned herself between him and the others. "Is your dream reliving an incident from one of your missions?"

"Yeah, so what?"

"I'm not trying to get under your skin," she'd said. "You probably have PTSD. You should see a therapist who can help you work through the trauma you experienced."

He'd frowned. "I'm fine. I don't need someone shrinking my head." He'd gripped her arms lightly and moved her to one side. "Now, if you'll excuse me, I going to get some of that sleep you think I'm missing."

As he'd passed by her, she'd touched his arm. "I work with a lot of guys just like you in my job at the VA. The problem doesn't just go away. All I ask is that you think about it."

She'd dropped her hand and stepped back. "I care about all the people who work with Jake, Cage and the rest of the team. You could be the one to have someone else's back. They need to know they can count on you." She'd smiled. "*I* need to know they can count on you." Then her smile had faded. "You need to know you can count on yourself."

Her words chose that moment to echo through his mind. Did he trust himself to handle a dangerous situation? His glance went to the two in the backseat. Did he trust himself to protect them without flaking out?

Hell, he hadn't flaked out yet. So, he didn't sleep worth a damn. That didn't make him crazy. Tired, yes. But not crazy.

At the very least, he could stay focused long enough to get them to Fool's Gold and Lost Valley Lodge. From there, Jake might decide to have one of the more seasoned men keep them safe until their situation could be resolved.

Short of killing Diego and the entire Valdez drug cartel, Venom wasn't sure their situation could be resolved. Unless they did like Garcia had suggested and created new identities.

If Jake did replace Venom as their protector, whom would he choose?

He glanced at Garcia as she brushed the tears off Sofia's cheeks and bent to kiss the tip of her nose.

His heart swelled inside his chest.

That mother loved her daughter.

Like the woman who'd loved her son in that Afghan village.

He barely knew them, but he couldn't imagine handing them off to someone else.

*Focus on the present,* he told himself.

"Where are we?" Garcia asked. "I'd check my cell phone, but I need to conserve the battery since I don't have a cord I can use to charge it."

"We're on Interstate twenty-five, fifteen minutes from Raton. Nearly to the border of Colorado."

"Mommy, can we stop to go to the potty?" Sofia asked.

"I'd planned to stop for food and gas in Raton. You can use the restrooms there. Can you wait that long?" He met Sofia's gaze in the mirror.

She nodded. "I think so. Can I have chicken nuggets?"

He glanced back at Garcia. "Mom?"

Her cheeks flushed. "Are you buying?"

Venom nodded, feeling her embarrassment at being beholden to others for everything, including feeding her child.

"I will pay you back as soon as I can get a job," she promised.

He could tell her pride was hurting. Rather than tell her she didn't have to, he said, "I'm not in a hurry."

"Good," she muttered. "I don't know how long it'll take to get back on my feet. Diego kept us locked up in the cartel compound in Mexico."

"How did you escape?" Venom asked.

"He allowed us to shop once or twice a year on

the US side of the border. I told him Sofia had to have new shoes, and she had to be with me to try them on. He agreed, sending one of his minions along with us with strict instructions to keep us in sight." She looked down at Sofia. "You want to tell him how we got away from Raul?"

The girl's face lit up. "We went to the bathroom in the mall. Raul couldn't come into the ladies' room. Mommy lifted me up to a window. I crawled through, and she lowered me to the ground. I landed on my feet." She grinned. "Mommy landed on her hands and did a somersault."

Garcia shrugged. "It wasn't as graceful as it sounds. I'd seen one of the guards fish a key from a magnetic box beneath the SUV. I banked on that box and key being there."

Venom frowned. "And if the key hadn't been there?"

"I was going to head for the train station, wait until dark and stow away in a box car."

His frown deepened. "And go where?"

"I didn't really care," she said. "Anywhere but El Paso."

He glanced at her reflection. "But you called JoJo."

Her lips twisted. "Do you believe in Fate, Kismet or just that things happen for a reason?"

He'd made it through too many close calls not to believe in something. Venom nodded.

"I was about to climb through that window when a woman entered the bathroom. When I told her I was escaping an abusive relationship, she offered to call the police."

"Why didn't you?"

Garcia shook her head. "The cartel's network is deep and extensive, including members of the police force."

"What about Fort Bliss? You were Army. Surely, you could have gotten help there."

"Sometimes, the gate guards are contracted and aren't military personnel. I didn't know who I could trust. I had to get us far away from El Paso on my own. Since I wouldn't let her call the police, she gave me her cell phone." Garcia smiled. "She told me to call someone to get help. Maybe a family member or a friend."

"Why didn't you call family?" he asked.

"My parents died in an auto accident. I don't have any siblings. There are some cousins in San Antonio, but I thought Diego would look there first." She shook her head. "He'd isolated me from any friends I'd had in El Paso, and that wasn't far enough away from him or the cartel. I had to dig deep to come up with a friend I knew would help."

"From what I've seen so far of JoJo, she'd do anything for someone she cares about," Venom said.

Garcia nodded. "JoJo and I deployed together in Afghanistan. I knew she went through a bad time there and would understand my need to get away. It took a minute to remember her talking about a lodge in Colorado and another minute to locate the town

on the other side of a pass from Colorado Springs."
She smiled.

"But you found it."

"And JoJo was there." She lifted her shoulders. "I
wouldn't have found JoJo without the kindness of a
stranger giving me her phone and insisting I call a
friend. There still are good people in this world. I'll
need to get her phone back to her once I get to Fool's
Gold. I owe her everything."

As Venom exited the interstate in Raton, Garcia
lowered her sunglasses, covering the bruise around
her eye.

Venom burned inside at the thought of that man
hitting Garcia.

As he pulled into a service station and parked
next to a gas pump, he turned to the woman in the
back seat. "You know, we've traveled a long way
together, and I don't even know your first name. JoJo
sent us on this mission to rescue her friend Garcia."

She laughed, her smile sending heat through his
body. "My given name is Maria Elena."

He studied her for a moment. "It suits you. But
it'll take a minute for me to quit thinking of you as
Garcia."

She smiled. "I don't mind if you call me Garcia. It
brings back some of the good memories I had of
serving in the Army."

"Then Garcia, it is. I'd prefer if you two stayed in
the vehicle until I'm finished getting gas. Then, we
can go inside together. If the drug cartel is as

powerful as I suspect, they probably sell all the way up to Denver, if not further."

Garcia nodded and turned to Sofia. "Can you wait a few more minutes?"

She nodded.

Venom hurried through the process of filling the tank, then moved the car to park at the side of the station. He held the door for Garcia and Sofia.

He leaned close to Garcia and whispered, "As far as anyone is concerned, we're just one happy little family on a trip." He took Sofia's hand in one of his, Garcia's in the other and walked with them into the convenience store and straight to the back to the restrooms.

He stood outside the ladies' room. "I'll be right here," he said and leaned against the wall.

Garcia frowned. "What about you?"

"I can wait," he said.

"For another two or more hours?" She glanced around the store. "We'll be okay for a few minutes." She grabbed his arm and turned him toward the men's room. "Go."

He didn't like letting them out of sight for a moment. It was bad enough that they would be in the ladies' room without him. "Is there a window in the restroom?" he asked with a crooked grin.

She shook her head, her lips pressing together. "I'm not ditching you. You got us this far. Besides, you have the key to the car. Hurry if it makes you feel better. We'll take a little longer."

When he hesitated, she waved toward the two doors. "We're right beside you. If we scream, you'll hear us."

Against his better judgment, he entered the men's room after Sofia and Garcia had gone through the other door. He relieved himself quickly, washed his hands and was back in the hall less than two minutes later.

He leaned close to the other door and called out, "You two still in there?"

When they didn't answer, he laid his hand on the door, ready to push through, but tried once more. "Maria, Sofia?"

The door opened suddenly, and he practically fell into Garcia. He grabbed her arms to steady himself, his body pressed against hers.

She laughed. "What are you doing?" Her hands settled on his hips, sending electric shocks throughout his body and pooling in his loins.

With his brain synapses firing left and right and his veins sending waves of molten blood through his system, he struggled to focus and say something that made sense. "I called out, and you didn't answer. I called out again when you opened the door."

"I already had my hand on the door handle, ready to respond quietly when I opened it. But you fell through." She looked up at him, her gaze meeting his, then sliding lower to his mouth. "Guess we didn't hear you the first time." As if she had just realized her hands were resting on his hips, she stepped back, a rosy flush creeping up her neck into her cheeks. "We were washing our hands…" Her voice trailed off.

Reluctantly, he released his hold on her arms, lowering his hands to his sides. "Sorry. I was worried."

"Can we get chicken nuggets?" Sofia tugged on Venom's arm, oblivious to the tension between the adults. "I'm hungry."

For a long moment, Venom met Garcia's gaze. What had just happened? He tore his gaze from hers and looked down at Sofia, looking up at him with those eyes that could make anyone do anything she asked.

He pulled himself together and nodded. "Let's get you those chicken nuggets before you shrivel up and blow away."

Her brow wrinkled. "I'm not going to shrivel up and blow away."

"Not if we get you something to eat," he held out his hand.

Sofia slipped hers into his and smiled up at him.

That smile and the tiny hand in his made him warm all over in an entirely different way than when her mother had touched him. The warmth the child inspired was a lot safer than the heat her mother stirred.

Venom was pretty sure that protecting an adult client did not include lusting after her. But there he was, smoldering inside, his groin tightening.

"Chicken nuggets," he murmured, bringing him

back to the task at hand. "Let's get this kid some food."

Sofia happily skipped along beside Venom.

Garcia trailed behind them.

Holding the mom's hand wasn't a good idea, the way he was feeling.

His job was to get Garcia and her daughter to Fool's Gold. After that, who knew what came next for the two?

It didn't make sense to get attached to the mother-and-daughter duo. They might not stay around long. Garcia had talked about moving on to a secret new life untraceable by the cartel. Knowing Hank and Jake, they could make that happen sooner than later. Hopefully, before Diego Valdez caught up to them. Until they bugged out, they'd need protection.

Venom wasn't sure he was the right man for the job. After his visceral reaction to her touch, he wasn't sure he could control his urge to hold her in his arms or quell his desire to do so much more.

How had the simple task of transporting a client and her daughter become so much more?

# CHAPTER 5

INSTEAD OF SLIDING into the back seat with Sofia, Maria settled her daughter and buckled her belt. She handed her the bag with her chicken nugget meal and closed the door.

Though she'd spent the last few hours staring into Venom's gray eyes reflected in the mirror, she hadn't been able to see much more of Venom's face. She felt a great connection with the man strictly based on eye contact. How could that have happened?

Was she falling for him because he was the man who'd showed up to rescue her and Sofia? Would she have felt the same if any other man besides Venom had shown up instead?

She slid into the seat beside him, glad to stare out the front window and avoid eye contact with Venom.

Maria was confused by his touch. No, that wasn't entirely true. She was turned on by his touch and disconcerted that the attraction had happened so quickly. Now wasn't the time to notice another man.

Having just left a bad relationship, she hadn't had time to decompress and learn to love herself first.

The years she'd wasted with Diego had whittled away at her confidence. His verbal abuse had been as destructive as his physical abuse.

Maria had been beaten in more ways than one. Making love with Diego had turned into rape. No matter how she'd felt, if he'd wanted sex, she hadn't had a say. They'd had sex, and she'd endured, hating him more with each passing day.

Then why this sudden interest in a man who was being paid to protect her, not make love to her?

Because Venom made her feel as if her thoughts and feelings mattered.

At the beginning of her relationship with Diego, he'd pretended to listen when she'd talked about her time in the Army, her dreams and her desire to go to college on the GI Bill to get a degree. Maybe she'd become an accountant or teacher.

When she'd agreed to move in with Diego, those dreams had screeched to an abrupt halt.

Everything she'd done had to be centered on him, leaving no time for herself, her continuing education or a career.

By the time she'd discovered she was pregnant, she'd given up on going to college. How could she when she would have a tiny baby to care for? She hadn't dared ask Diego to watch his own daughter while Maria attended classes. He'd refused to change a single diaper and had blamed her for letting herself get pregnant. Why hadn't she taken birth control?

She'd hoped the announcement of her impending motherhood would make him care more. Be more loving and less critical of everything she did.

If anything, her pregnancy had only made matters worse. He'd still talked down to her, making her feel worthless, and he hadn't hidden his disgust that she got fat as the baby grew inside her.

*Leave the past*, she reminded herself, *in the past.*

Venom slid into the driver's seat and shot a glance in her direction.

"Do you mind if I sit up here with you?" she asked.

"Not at all," he said and started the engine.

Maria turned to her daughter, who was more interested in the toy that had come with the child's nugget meal than eating the nuggets.

Sofia yawned, plucked a nugget from the bag and bit into it.

She was tired. After she filled her belly, Sofia would sleep. Hopefully, for the remainder of the journey.

Maria held the bag of hamburgers without opening it. Her gaze scanned the parking lot and beyond. As far as she was concerned, they still weren't out of reach of the Valdez cartel.

As Venom drove through the parking lot, Maria studied the people who'd stopped to top off their gas and grab a bite to eat. She tipped her chin toward a Hispanic man leaning on the corner of the building. "Was that guy there when we went in?" Maria tried not to stare openly at the guy, utilizing her peripheral vision instead.

"Yeah." Venom's jaw hardened. "That's a long time to be lurking on the side of the building." His eyes narrowed. "Could he be one of Diego's guys?" Venom asked.

"If he is, I don't recognize him. Then again, I only saw the men who lived or worked at the Mexican compound. Like I said, the Valdez Cartel could have people all along the routes heading north to sell their drugs. Diego only has to make a few calls and word spreads like wildfire."

Venom nodded. "I'll zigzag through the streets of Raton before I pop back onto the interstate heading north. If he's one of Diego's, he'll try to follow."

Venom drove slowly out of the service station.

Maria turned, pretending to look into the back seat at her daughter. "He's moving," she said. "He's getting into a gray car."

Venom's gaze shifted between the side and rearview mirrors. "It might be nothing. Let's see if he follows." Instead of taking the ramp onto the interstate, he turned in the opposite direction and drove deeper into the city of Raton, weaving his way through commercial and residential streets.

Swiveling in her seat, Maria muttered a curse under her breath. "He's back there."

At the next corner, Venom turned left in front of a large office building. He sped to the next corner, turned right and took another two rights, pulling through a dark alley toward the street with the large office building. He slowed, coming to a halt in the shadows.

A gray car drove by,

"That's him," Maria whispered, her heart racing. "What do we do?"

"Let's lose him," Venom said and backed through the alley to the street behind them, then drove through Raton, taking the less traveled roads. After a while, he pulled into a parking garage and parked.

"I think we lost him," Maria said. "Why are we stopping?"

Venom pulled out his phone and brought up the map. "I want to look at our options." He played with the map directions to Fool's Gold for a few minutes and shook his head.

"What?" Maria asked. "You don't look happy."

His lips twisted. "If we follow Interstate 25 all the way up through Colorado Springs, we can get to Fool's Gold in two and a half hours."

Maria drew in a deep breath and let it out. "His guy will report that he saw us. Since we were heading north on 25, he'll assume we'll keep heading north and seek other contacts to look for us. What else do you have?"

He nodded to the map. "If we avoid the Interstate, we more than double that time, depending on the way we choose to go. None of the alternate routes go straight there."

Her heart dove into her belly. "He won't give up. We have to take the long route."

Venom reached across the console and took her hand in his.

That spark of awareness shot through her system, spreading warmth to combat the icy feeling of dread Diego's reach created.

He squeezed her fingers gently. "What's so bad about adding a few hours to our trip, anyway? It's our family vacation." He gave her a half-hearted smile.

"That's right." She lifted her chin and matched his enthusiasm with some of her own. "So, we see a part of the country we wouldn't have seen from the inter-state." She frowned down at the map. "Which way do we go?"

He pointed to the east of Raton. "We can swing out east for a bit, then head north until we're parallel with Colorado Springs. The terrain is like this…wide open, no trees and you can see for miles."

Maria nodded. "More of the same thing we've been passing through since we left El Paso. What else have you got?"

"We could dip back to the south to Eagle's Nest and Red River and come up to the west of the moun-tain range. We'd pass the Great Sand Dunes National

Park and enter Fool's Gold from the west. If we take the eastern route, it's about five and a half hours. If we go west, we're doing some backtracking before we can head north again. It'll take about six and a half hours."

Maria's eyes narrowed. "An hour longer going west, but the scenery…"

He nodded. "You'll see forests, mountains and sand dunes."

"If the guy we just ditched is part of the Valdez network, he'll report that he saw us in Raton. Again, they'll assume we'll continue north, won't they?" She looked up into Venom's face.

He shrugged. "It would make sense. He probably got our license plate number as well."

Her heart skipped several beats. "Can he trace it to one of you in Fool's Gold?"

Venom shook his head. "Jake signed for it. I'm betting he took that into account. We can ask him when we get to Fool's Gold." He looked down at the map and back up into her eyes. "East? West? Or make a run for it straight up the middle?"

The temptation to hurry and get there warred with the need to get off the beaten path and not give Diego a clear picture of which direction she was headed.

She'd gone to the Red River ski resort with a church group when she'd been in high school. The mountains were beautiful. For the past five years, she'd been locked away in the cartel compound with only a few forays into El Paso for necessary clothes shopping.

"If we don't run into trouble, do you think we can stop at the Great Sand Dunes? I've always wanted to see them." She met Venom's gaze.

His lips curled upward. "As long as we're not being followed, we can make that happen. And we'll still get into Fool's Gold before midnight."

Maria faced the windshield. "What are we waiting for? The sooner we get going, the sooner we can be in Colorado."

"Are we almost there?" Sofia asked from the back seat.

"Not yet, *mija*." Maria shot a smile back at Sofia. "You might as well sleep. It'll make the trip seem shorter." Especially since they'd just more than doubled the time it would take.

"I'm not finished with my nuggets." Sofia held up a golden fried chicken nugget.

"Then finish up," Maria said. "After that, you can stretch out across the back seat—as long as you keep your seatbelt fastened."

Venom selected the western route on the map and followed the directions provided to get out of Raton on the road heading south toward Eagle's Nest.

Maria kept a vigilant watch for any vehicle that appeared to be following them. As they left Raton on the highway headed south to Cimarron, traffic thinned until they were practically the only car on the road. Maria settled back in her seat, giving her neck a break from craning over her shoulder.

Sofia had finished her food and argued that she was five and didn't need naps anymore. The little girl nodded off thirty minutes outside of Raton and stretched out across the back seat.

Mountains rose before them, giving Maria the first sense of peace she'd felt in a long time. For a moment, she let herself relax.

"How did you get mixed up with a drug cartel?" Venom asked.

Maria tensed at the mention of the cartel. Then she forced herself to let go of the worry, if only for a short time.

"You don't have to answer," he said. "It's none of my business."

She waved a hand. "I don't mind. It's like I was a different person back then."

"Trauma changes people," he said softly.

Maria glanced his way.

This Navy SEAL had experienced the horrors of war. He knew.

"Yes, it does," she agreed. "I was young, just separated from the Army and at a bar celebrating with friends. Diego was there—the most handsome man in the bar. You couldn't miss him with that dark hair and mysterious eyes. He walked straight up to our group, singled me out and asked me to dance." Her lips twisted. "I was flattered, smitten and stupid. For the next few months, we dated. He was kind, generous and wooed me into thinking he was perfect." She snorted. "God, I was blind. I thought I was in love with him. Looking back, I think I was in love with the idea of being in love. I ignored the signs that all was not right with him. We spent so much time together that he said it only made sense for me to move in with him." She shrugged. "So, I did."

"Did you know he was connected to a cartel?"

She turned to give him a grimace. "Not when I moved in. It became clear soon after. I was devastated. I thought I could save him from his family by convincing him to leave the business. We would run away together." She shook her head. "He didn't want out. How did I think he made money?" She laughed. "I'd never thought to ask. It was like I was living in a dream world that suddenly turned into a nightmare. I was sleeping with a man who was part of a drug cartel. And not just a little mom-and-pop cartel. The Valdez cartel was big and dangerous, with its tentacles stretching into the Mexican government and even into the US. They deliver drugs as far north as Canada."

"That had to be terrifying," Venom commented.

She nodded. "I wanted out. He wasn't the man I thought he was. I couldn't love a man who was responsible for delivering lethal drugs to kids."

"Why didn't you get out sooner?" he asked.

She smiled briefly. "Remember the part I've repeated about the Valdez family?"

"They don't let go of what they consider theirs." He shook his head.

"When I found out I was pregnant, I tried to leave. We were still living in his house in El Paso. I didn't get far before one of his henchmen caught up with me. They tied my wrists and ankles, stuffed me in the back of an SUV and drove me across the border into Mexico. They didn't let me out until we were securely inside the Valdez compound." Her lips pressed into a tight line. "That wasn't the first time Diego hit me. But it was bad. I thought I'd lose the baby. Diego made me feel like it would be my fault if I did. I shouldn't have run. I belonged to him."

"That bastard," Venom gritted out, his hands tightening on the steering wheel until his knuckles turned white.

"They kept me locked up on the compound until my first labor pains. Then they rushed me back across the border to the hospital in El Paso. I had my baby there."

Venom's brow furrowed. "Couldn't you have told someone at the hospital that you were being held hostage?"

Maria shook her head. "Diego told me that if I said anything to anyone, my baby would disappear. I'd never see her again. So, I stayed with him and put up with his abuse all those years because I thought he'd steal Sofia from me and I'd never see her again."

"What made you finally make a break for it?"

"He got mad at me a little over a week ago and started using me as a punching bag."

Venom cursed.

"As usual, I took it. But Sofia saw what was happening. She got between us and told Diego to stop." Maria gave him a sad smile. "She has a good heart. But Diego didn't see it that way. He back-handed her, sending her flying across the room. He'd never hit her before." She clenched her fists. "As I held her in my arms, I swore to myself he would never hit her again. Thus, the shopping trip, squeezing through a window and stealing the SUV."

"You're a brave woman, Garcia." He reached out and touched her cheek.

She covered his hand with hers, her fingers tightening around his. "I won't go back. And I won't let him take my baby."

"We'll make sure he doesn't get anywhere near you two," he promised.

He lowered his hand, taking hers with him. Through the mountains, past Eagle's Nest and Red River, he held her hand.

Maria liked that his hold was strong but loose enough she could easily pull away. Instinctively, she knew he'd never hold her down, hit her or lock her away from everyone she knew and cared about. This man was nothing like Diego.

If she wasn't tainted by her experience with the drug dealer, and if she wasn't on the run from the entire cartel, she might consider starting something with him.

If he was even interested. He was probably holding her hand out of pity.

She prayed that wasn't so. The last thing she wanted from Venom was pity.

Now, if he offered a kiss…

She'd consider a kiss. But nothing more, even if he tempted her. He deserved a woman with a whole lot less baggage.

Having been beaten down for years, Maria wasn't in any shape, physically or mentally, to start anything new. She had a long way to go to get right with herself first. After Diego, she hadn't been sure she would ever want a man touching her again.

But it would be nice to have someone to lean on when she was scared. Someone who would love her, even if she wasn't perfect. Maybe a man like Venom to hold her in his arms and make love to her gently. One who would consider her needs and desires.

The thought of making love with the Navy SEAL sent a flood of warmth to the coldest parts of her heart.

Venom might only be around to deliver her to JoJo. She'd be foolish to get too attached. If she had to go into hiding, she might never see him again.

Her belly knotted, and a lump lodged in her throat.

Maria couldn't think that far ahead. She had no

idea what her future would look like. Her fingers tightened around his ever so slightly.

When she'd been unhappily imprisoned in the Valdez compound, she'd learned to take the bad days one day at a time. She'd also vowed to take the good days one day at a time. Now, a little glimmer of hope built in her chest.

Though a pall of gloom hovered on the horizon, like the clouds building to the north, she chose to bask in a bit of happiness while it lasted.

God, she hoped it lasted.

# CHAPTER 6

"WE JUST PULLED into the Great Sand Dunes National Park to stretch our legs," Venom said.

"Glad you're making progress," Jake said. "It would've been nice for you to be at the lodge already, but I get it, given your encounter in Raton. Better to take the long way than to lead the cartel to the lodge."

Venom stood outside the ladies' room at the visitors' center, waiting for Garcia and Sofia to emerge.

Earlier, he'd notified Jake of the tail they'd picked up in Raton and their change in direction with the short stop at the Great Sand Dunes National Park. Since they'd chosen to travel a backroad, the park's visitors center provided a rest stop to stretch and give them a chance to use the restrooms. The added bonus was the amazing view of the white dunes.

Jake had just landed at the Colorado Springs airport and called to check on their progress.

"We still have three and a half hours to go,"

Venom said. "We should roll in between eleven and twelve o'clock tonight."

"I'll be there and awake," Jake said. "You have some weather moving in from the west. I have Swede tracking your cell phone in case you get into any trouble. Be careful on those curvy mountain roads. Rain makes them slick, and you never know what might step out in front of you." Jake laughed. "I almost hit an elk one night on the way back from Vail. I came around a blind curve, and he was just standing in the middle of the road. I slammed on my brakes, skidding to a stop less than a yard from him. He looked at me like he had no doubt I'd stop. Then he ambled off into the woods, unfazed."

Venom grinned. "I'll be sure to go slow on curves and look for large animals out for an evening stroll."

"How are you doing with Ms. Garcia?"

Jake's quick change in subject caught Venom off guard. "Great," he answered. Better than great. He was having lusty thoughts about the woman, and she'd just run from an abusive bastard who probably hadn't taken no for an answer.

"And the kid?" Jake asked.

"She's holding up better than I would've expected. Sofia seems to take everything in stride."

Jake chuckled. "Most kids are pretty resilient." He paused. "How about you? When we took off on this rescue mission, we only knew about one client. Not two. And we didn't know that second one was a child…"

"Yeah." Venom's hand tightened on the cell phone. "What's your point?"

"I've read your military file. I know about your last mission…and the…."

Venom closed his eyes.

*Don't say it.*

"…outcome," Jake said. "If working with this client and her daughter isn't what you signed up for, I can find someone to take over once you get them here." He paused for a moment, then added, "It's up to you. Either way, I'll understand."

At that moment, Sofia and Garcia emerged from the bathroom. The little girl skipped up to Venom and took his hand. "Mr. Vincent, can we see the dunes now?"

His heart swelled at Sofia's smile and inherent trust that he wouldn't hurt her. "We'll talk when we get there. Right now, I have to go."

Jake laughed. "Mr. Vincent, is it? I take it she's in charge now?"

"You've got that right." He met Garcia's gaze. "Out here." Venom ended the call and slid the phone into his pocket. "Jake made it to the airport at Colorado Springs."

Garcia let out a slow breath. "I'm glad. I seem to have disturbed your lives more than I intended. I had planned on driving Sofia and myself all the way to Fool's Gold. I hadn't considered a scenario where we'd meet halfway. I guess that's why you Brotherhood Protectors are needed. You think ahead. I just leaped first," she huffed, "out a window, no less. Then I scrambled to figure out what next."

"The important thing to remember is that you got away." He reached for her hand. "We don't have much time. Jake says there's weather moving in from the west. I suspect it will hit while we're still on the road."

"I know it was out of the way, but thank you for humoring us. Sofia's never been anywhere but El Paso and south of Juarez.

He dropped her hand to open the door for her. Once outside, she slipped her hand back into his as if that was where it belonged.

It felt right to have her hand in his and Sofia's little hand holding onto his finger.

They looked like just another family on vacation. Venom had never envisioned himself with a family. Yet, somehow, being with Sofia and Garcia felt strangely...right.

They only stayed for thirty minutes. Venom and Garcia were fully aware of the need to keep moving and cut their visit short. They still had a long way to go on curvy mountainous roads with few, if any, places to stop for the night should the weather get nasty.

Back in the car, they drove in silence for an hour.

Venom glanced over at Garcia. Her chin dipped toward her chest, and her eyes were closed. The stress of the day weighed on her. She had to be exhausted.

He second-guessed their decision to take the longest route. If they'd blown through on Interstate 25, they'd be at the lodge now.

And they'd have led the cartel straight to the mother and child escapees.

As painful as it was to take the long way, he felt confident they hadn't picked up a tail. In fact, the later the hour, the fewer vehicles on the road.

The clouds rolling in snuffed out the sunlight an hour earlier than the expected sunset.

The rental car's headlights came on automatically. Venom slowed a little, Jake's story about the elk making him hyperaware of the possibility of encountering wildlife on the road. They tended to come out after dark. He didn't have a lot of confidence that the car would provide much protection if they hit a full-size elk, bear or moose.

The rain started at the same time Venom reached the fork in the road where they would head east into a national forest and more mountainous terrain. The heavy rain held off until he started up a mountain. The droplets pelted the roof of the car and sounded like drumsticks tapping against metal.

The noise woke Garcia. "If it gets too bad, pull over and wait it out," she suggested.

He was one hundred percent on board with her sentiment. As much as he was ready to be there, he wouldn't risk their lives by making bad decisions. "I will."

Moments later, hail added to the noise, and

gusting winds blew it all sideways, pinging against the windows.

With the wiper blades working at maximum speed, Venom leaned forward and searched through the downpour for a place to pull off the road. Unfortunately, the road was only wide enough for the two lanes. Shoulders didn't exist. Metal guardrails gave a pathetic sense of security. They wouldn't begin to stop a two-thousand-pound vehicle from careening over the side of a cliff if the driver lost control and slammed into them.

Garcia pointed to the right. "There. Looks like an overlook pullout." She laughed. "Not that we can see anything, including the road in front of us."

"Mommy," Sofia called out from the backseat. "Are we going to crash?"

Garcia turned in her seat to face her daughter in the limited light from the dash. "No, baby. Mr. Vincent is going to stop for a while until the storm passes."

Venom eased off the road, praying the pullout was large enough to get them off the road without falling over the edge. There wasn't a guardrail marking the brink of the drop-off here. No matter how useless they were for keeping vehicles from flying off a ledge, guardrails were good for letting someone know where that edge was.

When he came to a stop, Venom shifted into park and let go of the breath he'd been holding.

"You'll have to peel your fingers off the steering wheel," Garcia said. "You had a death grip on it."

She was right. His knuckles were white. "It's been a long time since I've been caught in this heavy a deluge."

"I'm glad you pulled over. I couldn't see two feet in front of the windshield. I can't imagine you could see any better."

"Yeah. It came on faster than I anticipated." He leaned back and shook blood back into his fingers. "I figured stopping would be better than driving off a cliff."

She smiled. "Good call." Garcia unbuckled her seatbelt and turned sideways so that she could see her daughter without straining her neck. "Did you have a nice nap?"

Sofia nodded, flinching when lightning flashed, followed closely by a loud burst of thunder that rattled the windows. She pressed her hands over her ears. "I'm scared."

"Want to sit up here with us?" Garcia asked.

Sofia nodded, unbuckled her belt and climbed over the back of the seat as easily as only a little five-year-old could.

Rather than settle in her mother's lap, she slipped into Venom's and curled up against his chest, her little body shaking.

He opened his leather jacket and wrapped it and his arms around her, pulling her close.

She leaned her cheek against his chest and sighed.

Once again, Venom second-guessed their decision to take the long, scenic route. If they'd gone east of the mountain range, they might have missed the storm altogether, as well as getting in an hour earlier.

He glanced up to see Garcia staring at him and her daughter.

"Are you second-guessing this scenic route?" she asked.

He nodded.

She chuckled. "Me, too. Not that it does any good. We're here now." She stared at the rain-drenched windshield. "This storm will pass. We just have to make the best of it."

Venom's lips twitched. "Any suggestions on how to do that?"

For someone who'd been through five years of abuse, this woman wasn't going to let a little storm get her down. He was amazed at her resilience.

She cocked an eyebrow. "You could tell us a little more about yourself."

He stiffened. "You already know everything."

She snorted. "Hardly. I know you were in the Navy, you were a SEAL and you left before your twenty."

He opened his mouth to say he didn't want to talk about it.

She held up a hand. "Don't worry. I'm not going to ask about your time on active duty. I'm more interested in where you grew up."

He could talk about that without reliving hell. His childhood had been pretty good. "Galveston, Texas."

Her eyebrows rose. "You're a Texan?"

He nodded. "What about you?"

Her lips pinched. "El Paso. Other than when I was in the Army, I didn't stray far from my hometown."

"Will you ever go back there to live?" he asked.

She was shaking her head before he finished asking the question. "Never in a million years. I want to live where the temperatures don't get into the nineties by February and stay above ninety through October."

He laughed. "At least we had a breeze off the water on Galveston."

She smiled. "So, we have something in common."

He found her smile contagious and grinned. "We're both from Texas."

Garcia tilted her head to one side. "What did you like doing when you were a kid?"

Sofia looked up. "Did you like playing outside?"

Venom nodded. "I only came into the house at night or when it was raining. Although, sometimes, I played in the rain."

"What did you do outside?" the little girl in his arms wanted to know.

"I went fishing, built forts, rode my bicycle and climbed trees. In the summer, I spent most of my days on the beach, swimming, snorkeling, kite-surfing, kayaking and paddleboarding. When I was old enough, I went out on boats and jet skis with my friends. I love everything to do with water."

"Will you take me to the beach, Mr. Vincent?" Sofia turned her soulful eyes up at Venom.

Venom's chest tightened. The child's gaze hit him square in the feelings. He glanced over Sofia's head to her mother. "How does she do that?"

"What? Make you want to give her everything she ever asked for with just one look?" Garcia smiled. "She learned that before she turned two. Works on me, every time." Her brow furrowed.

"Me, too." Venom chucked Sofia under the chin. "There aren't any beaches in Colorado, sweet pea. But if we're ever near a beach, I'll take you there."

The wind wailed through the trees, whipping the rain against the side of the car.

Sofia leaned her cheek into his chest again and burrowed beneath his jacket. "I've never been to a beach. I want to build a sandcastle and play in the waves."

Venom smoothed back her hair from her forehead. "Do you know how to swim?"

She shook her head. "You can teach me."

Venom met Garcia's gaze.

"They didn't have a pool in the compound." Her gaze went to her daughter. "She knows about beaches because I read to her. Anything I could get my hands on. Books and magazines in both English and Spanish. I told her stories about the places I'd been while in the Army. She wants to go to all of them."

"What about school?" Venom asked.

Garcia's lips thinned. "Sofia's a smart girl. She could be in kindergarten now, but Diego refused to let her go. He insisted that I could homeschool her." She shrugged. "I did the best I could with what we had. She knows her numbers, letters and colors, and she can read a little."

Venom's arms tightened around Sofia. "Are you going to let her go to a public school?"

Garcia shrugged. "I don't know. I want her to have friendships and access to books and teachers who can help her learn and grow. I just don't know that I can leave her anywhere. Diego might seize the opportunity to grab her."

He understood. She'd find it difficult to let her daughter out of her sight. With his cartel network, Diego could find them and make good on his promise to steal Sofia away.

"What about you?" He cocked an eyebrow. "What did you like to do when you were a kid?"

Again, she stared out the window. "My parents didn't have much, but I never felt like I was missing anything." She smiled, the simple curve of her lips drawing his attention to them, making him wonder how soft they were.

"I rode my bicycle all over our neighborhood, played tag with my friends and camped out in our backyards. Though I was an only child, I grew up surrounded by other kids my age." Her brow furrowed as she shot a glance toward Sofia. "I want my daughter to have that."

Diego had taken that opportunity away from her by locking her in the compound.

If Venom had a little girl like Sofia, he would make sure she got to play with other children. "Is Diego her—"

"—father?" Garcia nodded. "Yet, he never was interested in raising a child. He was more interested in using her as leverage to keep me there."

"You never married?" He held up a hand. "You don't have to answer that. It's none of my business."

"It's okay," she said. "No. I thought when he asked me to move in with him, marriage would be the next step." She snorted. "He never asked. Not even when I became pregnant. By then, I didn't care. I wanted out." Her brow dipped, and she shot a glance his way. "I never thought to ask...are you..."

"Married?" he shook his head.

"Were you ever?"

Again, he shook his head.

"How is that possible?" Her cheeks suffused with a sexy blush. "I mean, well, look at you. You're good-looking..." She reached out and touched his bicep. "You've got all those...muscles, and you were a Navy SEAL. Women had to be throwing themselves at you." If possible, her cheeks turned even brighter red.

Venom laughed. "You make me sound like a celebrity. I'm not nearly as adept in socializing."

"Seriously, you can't tell me you didn't date."

"I did date. Once or twice, I thought it was serious, but being a SEAL took me away more often than I stayed. Those relationships didn't last. It was easier if I didn't get too attached. That way, neither party was disappointed when distance made us drift apart."

"So, that's another thing we have in common," she said softly. "Neither of us has been married." She stared at the rain pounding the windshield. "I was glad I hadn't married Diego. I can't imagine the nightmare of trying to get a divorce. I'm sure the cartel doesn't believe in divorce. Diego's father once said the only way out was feet up." She turned back to look at her daughter snuggled against Venom's chest, her brow crinkled and her eyes shadowed. "Whatever happens to me, I only want my daughter to be safe and happy."

Venom's gut tightened. "You're going to be safe and happy with her."

Her gaze shifted up to his. "I hope you're right." She tipped her head. "Do you hear that?"

He frowned. "Hear what?"

Her lips tilted upward. "Exactly. The rain is lightening."

While they'd been talking, the worst part of the storm had moved past. The rain had gone from thundering against the roof of the car to a light pattering. Finally, the windshield wipers could keep up, and Venom could see the road again.

"We should get going," he said. He hated to move

Sofia. She'd fallen asleep tucked into the warmth of his body and jacket.

"Let me take her." Garcia leaned close and slipped her hands between Sofia and Venom, her hands brushing against his chest in the process.

Her touch sent waves of a different kind of heat flowing through his body. Her face was close, her lips full and tempting.

When she looked up and caught him staring at her mouth, her eyes widened, and a flash of something, maybe awareness, darkened her brown-black irises. She hesitated in her effort to collect her child.

All Venom had to do was lean a little closer, and their lips would touch. As if drawn toward her like a magnet to metal, he felt himself swaying in her direction.

Sofia stirred and opened her arms, wrapping them around her mother's neck.

Venom sat back against the seat. The moment passed, the opportunity lost.

Though it hadn't happened, it didn't stop him from *wanting* to kiss her.

Part of him was glad for the interruption. Kissing Maria might have changed everything.

In order to protect her daughter, this woman could potentially be on a path to disappear.

Now was not the time to get involved.

Hell, they'd only just met.

And he was still suffering the effects of PTSD.

The trauma the mother and child had lived with

all those years would surely leave a mark. They needed time to heal. When Maria was ready, she'd need a man unencumbered with his own bullshit. A man who could protect them and be the rock they'd need in their lives to make them feel safe.

That man was not him.

As he waited for Maria to secure her daughter, his heart ached at that realization.

He could never be the right man for them.

Maria.

When had she made the shift from Garcia to Maria?

When he'd stopped thinking of her as a client or battle buddy and started seeing her as someone he could be with long after the mission was complete.

# CHAPTER 7

MARIA'S HEART fluttered as she gathered Sofia in her arms. For a split second, she could've sworn Venom had been about to kiss her. The thought shocked her and had her pulse racing and her breathing coming in ragged bursts, like her lungs couldn't figure out how to work normally.

What shocked her even more was that she'd wanted him to kiss her.

After living with Diego for five horrible years of sex without love, she didn't think she would ever want someone to touch her again, even with a simple kiss.

*Wow.*

Her breath hitched again as she held her daughter in her arms.

That desire for a kiss gave her hope for a future where she wasn't repulsed by a man getting close to her.

Maria stole a glance at Venom, and heat spread throughout her body. She could imagine Venom's hands on her, strong but gentle. Caressing, not controlling.

*Madre de Dios.*

Desire flared like a grass fire after years of drought.

"Mommy, are we there yet?" Sofia murmured.

"No, *chica*," Maria replied automatically, mentally dragging herself back to the task at hand. "We need to get you back in your seatbelt."

"I'm sleepy." Sofia screwed her fists against her eyes.

"I know, but you need to climb into the backseat and buckle your belt." Maria helped her daughter over the console and reached into the back to help her secure her belt. "Go back to sleep, *mija*."

Sofia was asleep before Maria settled into her own seat and buckled her seatbelt.

Venom shifted into drive and pulled out onto the rain-soaked road.

Neither adult spoke as they continued along the curving road through the mountain pass.

Venom drove slower than the recommended speed limit, carefully rounding each curve.

Maria stole glances in his direction.

Was she so starved for the love of a good man that she was falling all over herself over the first one to show her kindness?

She faced forward, struggling to bring her racing pulse and runaway imagination under control.

After five years of having someone else dictate her life for her, she had to get right with herself before she even considered letting herself entertain the idea of falling in love again.

She'd thought she was in love with Diego. And where had that gotten her?

No. Love and relationships were out for now. If she could get to a point where she and Sofia were safe, she needed to concentrate on providing a warm, loving and secure environment for her daughter. Introducing another person into their world would complicate their lives more than they needed.

So caught up in her thoughts, Maria didn't register what was happening right in front of them until Venom jammed on the brakes and muttered, "Holy shit."

A huge tree crashed across the road and slid over the other side and down a steep embankment along with half the upper hillside in a sea of mud, boulders and vegetation.

Maria braced her hands on the dash. "What the hell?"

"Landslide." Venom slammed the gearshift into reverse, looked over his shoulder and backed up as fast as he could, but not quickly enough. The tires spun and sank as they were caught in more of the hillside, sliding down the mountain.

"Hang on," Venom said through gritted teeth.

Hanging on was all she could do as mud and debris lifted the car and carried it over the edge of the road and down an embankment like a raft navigating Class VI river rapids.

Maria held onto her armrest, unable to turn and check on Sofia in the back seat. The car bucked and twisted on the way down the hillside, bouncing off boulders and massive tree trunks.

Maria closed her eyes and prayed they wouldn't flip over or get buried beneath the mud and debris. Her seatbelt held her against the back of the seat. She had no idea what was happening to Sofia. As small as she was, she could slip out of her seatbelt and be tossed around like a ragdoll.

Venom's hand reached out and grabbed Maria's arm, holding her steady as they slid down the hillside for what seemed like an eternity.

Eventually, the slope leveled out, and the river of mud carrying them slowed until the car came to a stop, wedged between a tree trunk and a boulder.

The front of the car tilted upward, the headlights pointing up the hill. Though they were covered in mud, they produced just enough light that Maria could see more mud and debris flowing steadily toward them. It was moving slowly, but the mud was building up around them.

Venom unbuckled his seatbelt. "We have to get out of the car," he said, his voice tight.

"Into that?" Maria shook her head. "We'll be swept away."

"If we don't get out, we'll be buried alive." He reached into the back seat. "Sofia, are you okay?"

"Mr. Vincent, I bumped my head," Sofia whimpered.

Maria released her buckle and started to turn to comfort her child.

"Maria, see if your window will lower," Venom called over his shoulder.

At the angle the car tilted, her window was highest up in the mud slurry. With the lights still shining, she knew the battery was still working. She pressed the button on the side of the door.

The window lowered halfway and stopped.

Venom had started to pull Sofia into the front seat. He stopped. "Stay back here and cover your eyes."

He turned to Maria. "Get on the floorboard and cover your face and neck."

She didn't argue or ask questions. Instead, she slid off the seat onto the floorboard and covered the back of her neck.

Venom laid on his back over the console and cocked his leg. "Close your eyes," he ordered.

Maria shut her eyes.

A moment later, a loud crash sounded, and bits of glass rained down over her back and hair.

Venom kicked at what was left of the window. Then his hand touched her shoulder.

"Maria, you first." He gripped her hand and pulled

her up beside him. "Climb up on top of the roof. I'll hand Sofia up to you."

She nodded, slipped through the window and clambered onto the car's roof. It was too slippery to stand on, so she spread out on her belly and reached down. "Ready," she said.

The mud had risen, covering one of the front headlights. Before long, it would be over the other, and they'd have no light.

Sofia popped through the window, reaching her little arms up.

Maria hooked her beneath her arms and scooted backward, dragging her onto the car's roof. As soon as she had Sofia safely on top of the car, she moved them both toward the rear.

Venom's head and shoulders appeared. He pulled himself out of the car and up onto the roof.

Although the rain had slowed to a drizzle, it quickly soaked through Maria and Sofia's clothes that they'd worn for the warm, dry weather of El Paso.

Venom pushed to his feet, shot a glance at the front of the car and turned to study their situation. The only things not submerged in the mud were the top of the tree and the huge boulder. "We don't have much time left before the mud covers the last headlight. Maria, if I give you a boost, do you think you could make it to the top of the rock?"

She looked up. The rock was taller than she was by

a foot or more. With his help, she'd make it happen. Staying on top of the car, which was quickly becoming engulfed in mud, wasn't an option. "I should be able to."

Maria set Sofia at arm's length. "I'm going first. You'll come after me. Mr. Vincent will take care of you." She kissed her forehead. "You're a big girl. You can do this."

Sofia nodded, released her hold around Maria's neck and crawled across the car roof to Venom.

"Hold onto my leg," he said, "and don't let go."

She wrapped both arms around his left leg and held on tight.

Venom bent, cupped his hands and nodded to Maria.

Maria stared up at the rock, slick with rain. She drew a deep breath, let it out, then placed her foot into his palms. As she stepped up, she reached for the top of the rock, feeling along its jagged surface for a handhold. She found one, but it didn't do much good. Without enough strength in her arms, she couldn't pull herself up.

Venom straightened, lifting her higher until she could lay her belly over the top of the rock and swing up her leg.

A hand landed on her ass and gave her a gentle push.

Maria rolled over and lay with her face to the sky. Heavy mist coated her arms and cheeks. With no time to contemplate the clouds, she turned onto her stomach and reached for Sofia.

Venom handed her daughter up.

As soon as she had Sofia safely on top of the giant boulder, she moved back and waited for Venom.

As he pulled himself over the edge, she reached down, grabbed his belt and helped drag him the rest of the way to the top.

By the time he was lying across the summit, mud had slid over the last headlight, extinguishing what little light was left.

Maria pulled Sofia into her arms.

Venom pulled off his leather jacket and wrapped it around both of them. He sat behind Maria and pulled her against him, wrapping his arms around her and Sofia.

Sofia curled into Maria's wet shirt, shivering. "I'm cold, Mommy," she said, her teeth chattering.

Though she tried not to, Maria shivered as well. "I know, baby."

They'd escaped hell in Mexico and survived a landslide. Maria wondered if they'd succumb to hypothermia before anyone found them.

As cold as she and Sofia were, she couldn't imagine how Venom was holding up after giving up his leather jacket for them.

The man behind her leaned back. "If she's still cold, put her between us."

Maria turned and faced Venom.

He positioned her legs over his thighs and scooted her and Sofia closer until Sofia's back pressed against his chest.

Venom slid his arm beneath the jacket and hugged Maria closer, sandwiching Sofia between them, effectively shielding the child from the drizzle and warming her with their combined body heat.

Used to the heat of El Paso, Maria didn't know how long she'd last in the damp chill of a night in the Colorado Rocky Mountains. She shivered, even with the jacket protecting her from the elements.

Venom's hands rubbed across her back, but it wasn't enough to dispel the chill sinking all the way to her bones.

Maria leaned her forehead against his chest, the cold and constant shivering making her sleepy. She drifted in and out of consciousness, shivering until she didn't shiver anymore.

How long they stayed like that, she wasn't sure. Eventually, she blinked her eyes open. The drizzle had stopped, clouds had parted, and starlight shined down on their rock.

"Hey, Maria." Venom extracted an arm from around her and brushed a damp strand of wet hair off her cheek.

"So, now it's Maria?" Was it because they were going to die that he chose now to be more personal?

"Yeah," he said. No explanation.

She was too tired to demand one. Instead, she leaned her face into his neck, liking his woodsy scent. "Are we there yet?" she asked, her voice not much more than a whisper.

He leaned forward, his breath warm against her temple. "No, we're not."

Were those his lips against her skin? Had he brushed a kiss across her forehead? What would he do if she lifted her face to him? Would he take that kiss to her lips? Maria raised her head. His face was close enough. All he had to do was move maybe an inch.

His gaze dropped to her mouth.

For a moment, Maria thought he would kiss her.

Then he lifted his head. "If we want out of here, we'll have to do it ourselves."

"No mountain rescue teams?" The thought of moving seemed an impossibility.

He shook his head. "No. But I think we can make it out to the road."

She snorted. "It's covered in half a hillside."

He nodded in the direction behind her. "I can see a road below. If we can make it there, we can follow it until we find shelter."

Maria was tired to the bone, having expended every ounce of energy shivering. And she was a little disappointed Venom hadn't kissed her. If they died of exposure that night, would he regret not taking that chance?

She sure as hell would.

Then again, he was right to focus on what was more important. No one knew where they were. So, they had to rescue themselves. And if there were a chance to get Sofia somewhere warm and dry, Maria would push a little harder to make it happen.

Venom moved her legs off his. His hands were warm against her wet jeans. Too bad her skin was too numb with cold to feel the strength of his fingers.

Once he'd extricated himself, he stood and offered her a hand up.

Stiff from cold and weighed down by a sleeping Sofia, Maria couldn't help herself. Venom practically lifted both of them until Maria could stand on her own, Sofia tucked inside his leather jacket.

She turned and peered through the tree branches to a narrow ribbon of road bathed in starlight.

The rock they'd landed on was tall and as long as a school bus.

Venom strode to the opposite end. "I think we can get down from here," he said.

Maria joined him, carrying Sofia.

The other end of the giant boulder leaned against a higher slope than the one the landslide had flowed down. If they were careful, they could descend that slope to the road below.

Venom stepped off the rock and onto the slope. He turned and held out his hands. "I'll carry Sofia."

Maria peeled her daughter's arms from around her neck and handed her over, pressing a kiss to her cool cheek.

Sofia only moaned and melted against Venom without opening her eyes.

"She's beyond exhausted," Maria said, her heart

aching. Again, she wondered if she'd done the right thing.

"We'll get her somewhere safe and warm," Venom promised.

God, she hoped so. In the meantime, she shrugged out of his leather jacket. "You'll need this to keep her warm."

He frowned. "You'll get cold."

"Sofia will get colder. I'll be moving to stay warm." She stepped across to the hillside and held the jacket open.

He inserted one arm while balancing Sofia in the other. Once he had the jacket on, he zipped it over Sofia's back. Then he turned to Maria. "Let's get out of here."

"I'm all for it." She wrapped her arms around her middle and started down the steep slope, placing her feet carefully on the wet ground. They couldn't afford to slip and fall. Sofia's life depended on both of them staying alive.

Starlight shone down on them, making it easier for them to see where they were going.

Venom led the way, guiding her around obstacles, avoiding drop-offs and taking her down the most accessible slope he could find.

At one point, she'd slowed until the gap had widened to a couple of yards between them. When she increased her speed to catch up, she slipped on loose rocks, landed hard on her backside and slid on her butt, closing the distance between them before she came to a stop.

"Are you all right?" he asked as he reached down and pulled her to her feet. He used a little more force than she was ready for, and she crashed into him.

Venom's arm slipped around her waist, holding her against his side until she was steady on her feet.

He leaned close to her ear. "You're amazing."

She laughed. "Because I can descend a mountainside on my butt?"

"No, because you're brave, determined and care so much about your daughter, you'd risk your life for her. And even though you're so tired you can barely stand, you press on." He brushed his lips across her forehead.

Her heart swelled, warming her from the inside out. She lifted her head, wishing that kiss had landed on her lips.

He stared into her eyes for a long moment, then bent lower and captured her mouth with his.

The kiss was brief, but it left her head spinning.

Sofia stirred beneath the jacket, bumping against Maria and breaking the spell.

Venom's arm remained around her waist. "Can you go on?"

She nodded.

He lowered his arm slowly, making sure she could stand on her own. After another long look, he turned and started down the slope.

Maria's tongue swept across her lips. She could

swear she tasted his mouth. Her gaze followed his broad shoulders as he descended lower.

When she realized he was getting further and further away, she followed, her head in a daze. She wasn't sure whether it was the altitude or the kiss.

No, she was sure…it was the kiss.

If they got off that mountain alive, she hoped he would do it again.

After an eternity of trudging slowly down the side of the mountain, they finally reached the road below.

"Is this the same highway we were on?" Maria asked.

"Yes," Venom looked right and then left. "Only I think we're on the east side of the mountain pass."

She hugged herself around her middle, wishing for a blazing fire to warm herself by. "East…west…" Too tired to think, she shrugged. "Is that closer to Fool's Gold or further away?"

He smiled. "Closer."

"Good, I'm ready to be there." She knew it was still a very long way, especially on foot. But there had to be houses and people along the way who could give them shelter and let them use a telephone.

Maria still had the cell phone the woman in the bathroom had loaned her, but the battery had long since died. She was pretty sure Venom's cell phone was somewhere inside the ill-fated rental car, buried in mud. Not that they would get reception up in the mountains.

"This road is lower than the one we were driving

on," she said. "Does that mean we're on the way down the mountain now?"

"Let's hope so." With one arm around Sofia, Venom reached for Maria's hand.

She placed her palm in his warmer one and leaned into his shoulder as they walked down the road.

They'd been walking for a while when a light shone around a curve ahead.

Maria's heart sped up. "Someone's coming."

Venom drew her to the side of the road and waited on the straightaway for the vehicle to round the curve and find them in the beam of their headlights.

As the headlights came into view, Maria stepped behind Venom, her hand on his arm, a horrible thought coming to mind. "You don't think it's the cartel, do you?"

"No one knows where we are," Venom reminded her. Still, he remained in front of her as he waved at the approaching vehicle.

It slowed to a stop a few yards away from them, and the door flew open.

The driver got out.

With the headlights blinding her, all Maria could see was the silhouette of a man as he stepped away from the vehicle and headed toward them, limping slightly.

"Venom?" a deep voice called out.

Venom raised a hand to shade his eyes against the

glare of the headlights. "Jake?"

The man hurried forward. "Holy hell, man, where's Miss Garcia and the child?"

Maria stepped up beside Venom as he unzipped his jacket, revealing her sleeping daughter.

The other doors opened. Another man and a woman dropped down and hurried forward. The woman carried a blanket. As she stepped into the light, Maria's eyes filled. "JoJo."

"Garcia, what the hell happened? Why are you on foot?" She wrapped the blanket around Maria's shoulders and rubbed them hard. "You're frozen."

"Let's get all of you into the SUV," the other man said. "You can fill us in once you're thawed out."

JoJo slipped an arm around Maria's shoulders and led her to the SUV. Venom carried Sofia still tucked inside his jacket. The man with JoJo climbed into the back seat, leaving the middle seat open for JoJo, Maria and Sofia.

Venom waited for Maria to get into her seat and buckle her seat belt before he handed over Sofia.

JoJo settled the little girl between them, secured her seatbelt and then laid the blanket over her and Maria before settling in on the other side of Sofia.

After the women were secured, Venom climbed into the front passenger seat beside Jake. Once all the doors were closed, Venom turned up the heater.

Maria closed her eyes and leaned her head back against the headrest. Wrapped in a blanket, with heat flowing around her, she smiled. "Did I die and go to heaven?"

JoJo laughed. "No. You're very much alive but as close to heaven as you can get. You're in the Colorado Rocky Mountains."

"JoJo?" Maria whispered, on the verge of passing out.

"Yes, Garcia?" JoJo responded.

"Thank you for sending the cavalry to save us."

"That's what friends are for," JoJo said.

Safe inside a warm vehicle with good people around her to look after her and Sofia, Maria let go of consciousness. She'd worry about the rest of her life tomorrow.

# CHAPTER 8

"I DON'T KNOW how you three survived that landslide." Jake stared at the television in the corner of the dining room as he sat across the table from Venom.

The Denver news channel had sent a helicopter out to film footage of the landslide that had buried a portion of a highway in the mountains west of Fool's Gold. The reporter zoomed in on what appeared to be the front end of a car sticking out of the mud at the bottom of the slide, most of it buried. A check with the local sheriff's department revealed that the passengers had escaped unharmed.

The images flashing across the screen displayed the full extent of the damage. Half a hillside had broken loose in the torrential rain and slid down the side of the mountain, decimating trees, dislodging boulders and sending tons of mud down a wide swath. A portion of the highway was buried beneath twenty feet of mud and debris, forcing the road to be closed indefinitely until the highway department could safely move the blockage.

Venom shook his head, as amazed they survived as Jake. "We were lucky."

Jake grinned at Venom. "That was one hell of a first assignment as a Brotherhood Protector. Good job."

Venom frowned. "It's not over."

"True," Jake said. "But now that you have her and her daughter here, you don't have to continue. I can assign another man to take it from here."

Venom's frown deepened. "What happens next with them?"

Jake met Venom's gaze. "Hank and Swede have done more research on the Valdez Cartel. They're one of the largest cartels along the border, and their drug supply operations stretch all the way up into Canada. Which means they have eyes and ears all along the way. That's why they were able to spot you in Raton."

"How do you know that tail was them?"

Jake's lips twisted. "Hank's got a friend in the DEA. They've been tracking the Valdez cartel for a while. They're working toward a secret sting operation and have a couple of men on the inside. They heard the call go out to be on the lookout for Diego's woman and his child, and they also heard the call when one of their guys in Raton spotted them."

Venom's fingers clenched into fists. "So, she was

right. They have an extensive network. How can we protect her from it?"

"We?" Jake met and held Venom's gaze. "Does that mean you want to continue this assignment? You made us promise not to have you protect children. And my apologies, I didn't know Miss Garcia had a child."

"What's done is done." Venom waved his hand. "After all they've been through, they need some sense of stability. Switching protectors now will undermine their trust." He inhaled and let the air out slowly. "I want to stay with them until the situation is resolved."

"Or the DEA puts them into some kind of witness protection. She's bound to know things about the cartel they could use."

Venom shook his head. "Diego kept her a prisoner in their Mexican compound. I doubt she had access to their drug trafficking business."

Jake shrugged. "Even if the DEA won't help her into the witness protection program, Hank has connections with people who could set her and Sofia up with an all-new life, far away from the Valdez Cartel. In which case, you'll just be responsible for her and the child until she *disappears*."

"And then what happens to them?" Venom asked. "Who will provide for their protection?"

"If they disappear without entering the witness protection program, they'll be on their own. No one should be able to find them."

Venom didn't like the idea of Maria and Sofia hiding out in some little town with no one looking out for them.

"In the meantime," Jake said, "they can stay here until we can transfer them to the safe house."

Venom's brow rose. "We have a safe house?"

Jake nodded. "Hank has had people working on it for almost a year. It's finally finished and ready to use. Hank wants to move them in as soon as they're ready."

"Where is this safe house?" Venom asked.

"If I tell you…" Jake grinned.

Venom shook his head. "You'd have to kill me."

The man's grin broadened. "No, but I'll have to show you where it is. Since you'll be going with them, you have a need to know where it's located. It's actually kind of cool."

"Let me know when you want to go." Venom pushed back from the table, gathered his breakfast plate and Jake's and headed for the kitchen.

"Leave them in the sink," a gruff voice called out. Gunny Tate, hot pad in hand, opened an oven and peered inside. "Five more minutes," he murmured and closed the oven door.

He turned to Venom. "Saw the news." Gunny shook his head. "You did an amazing thing living through that landslide."

"Maria and Sofia were the ones who were amazing, considering what they've been through in the past twenty-four hours." He laid the dishes in the sink. "Now, if you'll excuse me, I want to check on them."

"You might want to take a cup of hot cocoa up to them. I have some made." Gunny crossed to the stove, stirred the contents of a pot and poured it into two mugs. Then he dropped a handful of mini marshmallows into each and placed the cups on a tray.

"Let me know if I need to send a breakfast tray up to them," Gunny said. "They need to eat but might want to lay in bed a little longer."

"Thanks, Gunny." Venom left the kitchen carrying the tray with the two mugs. He hurried through the dining room, where Jake was finishing his cup of coffee and climbed the stairs to the second floor.

JoJo had assigned Maria and Sofia to the room beside Venom's, knowing he was the Brotherhood Protector safeguarding the pair.

Venom stood outside their room, glad for the cocoa giving him as good an excuse as any to knock.

Carefully balancing the tray in one hand, he knocked with the other.

"Come in," Maria called out.

He twisted the door handle and pushed the door open.

Maria sat on the side of the bed, a frown furrowing her brow as she stared at Sofia, lying still in the bed. When she glanced up, her gaze made Venom's chest tighten.

He set the tray on a table and hurried forward to take her hand in his. "What's wrong?"

She pressed her fingers to her daughter's brow. "She's running a fever, and she's very lethargic." Maria looked up into Venom's eyes. "I'm worried. Sofia's never lethargic."

"Has she woken up at all?"

Maria raised her shoulders. "She moaned a couple of times in the night, but she hasn't gotten up. I figured the moaning was her having nightmares about running from El Paso or the landslide. Now, I'm not so sure. I'd feel a whole lot better if she woke up."

"Have you tried to get her up?" he asked.

"I sat her up, and she looked around the room and asked, *Are we there yet?* When I said yes, she tipped over, went back to sleep and hasn't woken again." Maria chewed on her bottom lip. "I don't know what to do."

"How high is her temperature?" he asked, his gut tightening. He'd seen Sofia as the sharp firecracker of a five-year-old, lighting up the inside of the car with her personality. The little girl lying in bed, her face pale and her eyes closed, frankly terrified him.

What if she was sick? Bad sick?

Despite the danger of discovery by the cartel, Sofia could be in more danger of a life-threatening medical issue. Refusing to get help could exacerbate the problem and send her into a downward physical spiral.

*Whoa.*

He was panicking over something that had yet to

happen and hopefully wouldn't. Venom leaned over the bed and brushed a strand of hair off Sofia's forehead. Her skin was warm to the touch.

"I'll find a thermometer." Venom ducked out the door into the hallway, turned and headed for the bedroom assigned to JoJo.

After only one knock, JoJo pulled open the door with one hand while trying to button her shirt with the other. "Venom, can I help you?"

"Do you have a thermometer? Sofia has a fever."

"Yes, sir," JoJo said. "What kind do you need?"

"What kind?" he asked, his brow dipping low.

"Dog, meat, candy or human?" JoJo listed.

Venom never knew there were so many types of thermometers. "Human."

JoJo frowned, spun and marched into her adjoining bathroom. Metal hinges squeaked. JoJo called out, "Ha. Found it." She appeared in the bedroom, carrying a hand-held device like the ones they used in the doctor's office.

"It's a battery-powered thermometer," she explained. "You wave it over her forehead slowly, while holding down the button." She placed it in his hand. "Let me know how she is. We don't have any children's anti-inflammatory medications, but I could run into town and pick up what we need at the pharmacy."

His fingers curled around the thermometer. "Thanks." He ducked back through her door and hurried back to Maria.

She took the thermometer and turned it on. Then she pressed the button and moved it slowly over Sofia's forehead. When she finished, she turned to read the display.

Her brow furrowed.

"What is it?"

"She's burning up. She's got a temperature of 104 degrees." Maria set the device on the nightstand and pulled the blankets off Sofia. The child wore a T-shirt with the words *I won't come if I can't bring my dog* written across the front. Probably a loner from JoJo whose dog had free range of the lodge.

"We have to get her body cooled down," Maria said. "We'll need a cool, damp cloth and something like an anti-inflammatory to bring the fever down."

"I'll be right back." Venom ran out into the hallway.

JoJo was headed his way. "How is she?"

"Running a high temperature. We need something to bring it down."

JoJo nodded. "Max is in town picking up supplies. I'll have him stop at the pharmacy on his way back for some children's Ibuprofen." She pulled her cell phone out of her pocket and pressed the number at the top of her favorites list. "Max, are you heading back soon? Good. I need you to run by the pharmacy and pick up some children's Ibuprofen. Great. Thanks." She ended the call and nodded. "He was about to head back. It will only take a few minutes for him to stop by and pick up what we need. He should be here soon."

"Thanks." His heart pounding in his chest, Venom raced back to Maria's room and ducked into the bathroom. He wet a cloth with cool water and squeezed most of the water out before taking it into the bedroom.

Using a magazine, Maria was fanning Sofia's body where she lay on top of the blankets. When Maria saw him coming, she met him halfway across the room and took the cloth from his hand. She laid it over Sofia's forehead. It didn't take long for the cloth to grow warm.

"JoJo's fiancé, Max, is stopping at the pharmacy for ibuprofen. He should be here in the next fifteen minutes," Venom said.

"Good. Maybe that will help." Maria lifted the washrag off her daughter's forehead and waved it in the air to cool before laying it across one of the child's cheeks.

Sofia stirred. A tear slid from the corner of one of her eyes, and she whimpered softly.

Venom stood at the foot of the bed, his heart breaking for the little girl. "What can I do?"

"Hold her hand...talk to her... She likes you." Maria carried the cloth into the bathroom to wet it again.

Sofia released a shaky sob, more tears slipping from the corners of her eyes, making wet spots on the pillowcase.

Venom rounded the end of the bed and lifted Sofia's hand. "Hey, hotshot." What did he say to an unconscious kid?

*Anything.*

"Can't lay around forever, you know. We have adventures waiting for us. I have to teach you to swim. Oh, and I need a fishing buddy. I was hoping that would be you. What do you say? Have you ever gone fishing?"

When she didn't respond, he kept going. "You'll need a fishing pole, and we'll have to dig up some worms. I'm sure there are a lot around the barn. Did you know they have horses here? I bet RJ can teach us how to ride. I never learned how to ride a horse, but I'm willing to try if you are."

Maria returned with the cool, damp cloth and laid it across Sofia's forehead.

Sofia's sobs had stopped along with the tears. Encouraged, Venom lowered his voice. "Did you know that JoJo has a dog? His name is Roscoe. He likes people food better than his dog food. I bet he would love to play. He has a ball JoJo throws for him, but he doesn't bring it back. Maybe you could teach him."

Venom took a deep breath, scrambling for something else to say.

He looked at Maria as she applied the cold compress to Sofia's forehead again and then across her chest.

"Is she cooling off?" he whispered.

"Give her a minute, and I'll check," Maria said. "If this doesn't work, we'll have to put her into a tepid bath."

"And if that doesn't work?" he asked.

"It better," she said, pressing her lips together. "Otherwise, we'll have to take her to a hospital emergency room. Running a high fever for too long is bad." She stood with the cloth in her hand, lines of worry etched across her forehead.

He took the cloth and went to the bathroom to rinse it in cool water. When he returned, Maria sat in a chair beside the bed, holding her daughter's hand and talking softly.

"Gonna need you to get better soon, *mija*. We have a lot to do. We need to find a place to live with a room just for you. Maybe we can paint your room. You'll have to think about what color you'd like. My favorite color is blue." She leaned over and kissed her daughter's cheek. "I'll need your help painting."

Venom approached the other side of the bed and laid the cloth across Sofia's forehead. Moments later, the cloth was warm. As Maria had done, he lifted it, fanned briefly and laid it across her cheek.

Maria reached out and caught his hand. "Let her body regulate without the cool, damp cloths for a minute. Then, I want to recheck her temp."

He nodded and held the cloth, fanning to cool it.

A couple of minutes passed before Maria lifted the thermometer and passed it over Sofia's forehead.

When she read the numbers, she didn't say anything; she just turned it toward Venom.

It hadn't changed. She was still showing 104 degrees.

They continued to apply the cool compresses, holding out for the ibuprofen.

When Max arrived, JoJo met him downstairs and ran all the way up with the bottle of liquid children's ibuprofen.

Maria read the dosage instructions, measured what Sofia needed into a plastic syringe and carried it to the bed.

Venom slipped his arms behind Sofia and lifted her to a sitting position.

She moaned and blinked her eyes open. "Mommy?"

"Yes, *chica*, I'm here," Maria said. "I need you to take this medicine. It will make you feel better." She held the plastic syringe to her daughter's lips. "Open up and swallow," she said and squirted the liquid into Sofia's mouth.

Some of it dribbled down her chin, but she managed to swallow the rest.

Maria held a glass of water with a straw to Sofia's lips. "Drink some water, *mija*. It will help."

Her daughter sucked on the straw, then pushed it out of her mouth and let her head loll back against Venom.

He brushed a kiss across her forehead and eased her down on the mattress, arranging her pillow beneath her head. "Sleep, princess. You'll feel better soon."

"Will you stay with me, Mr. Vincent?" she whispered without opening her eyes.

He reached for her hand and held it gently in his. "You bet I will. I'll be here as long as you need me."

She raised his hand to rest against her cheek.

Venom settled into the chair beside the bed and held Sofia's hand. For how long, he didn't know. He'd left his watch in his room, and his cell phone was buried in a car beneath a mountain of mud.

He didn't really care what time it was. It didn't matter. What did matter was getting Sofia's fever down. Her hand was hot in his.

Fifteen minutes passed and stretched into thirty. An hour later, Maria ran a temperature check and shook her head. "I'm going to run a bath. When it's ready, we'll carry Sofia into the bathroom and lay her in it. I don't like doing it, but I don't want the fever to fry her brain and internal organs."

Maria entered the bathroom. She turned on the faucet and let it run. After a while, the water was shut off, and Maria stood in the doorway to the bathroom, grimacing. "She's not going to like this any more than I like doing it."

Venom stood, gathered the little girl in his arms, and carried her into the adjoining bathroom. He stared down at the requisite tepid water and cringed. Knowing how miserable it was to lay in cool water, he fought an internal battle.

Maria settled the conflict by pulling Sofia's shirt over her head, taking her from Venom's arms and settling her into the water.

As soon as she hit the water, she cried out.

"I'm sorry, *chica*," Maria said. "You have a fever. We have to cool you down."

Sofia settled into mournful sobs as her mother swished the tepid water over her body.

Venom stood back, wanting to pull that baby out, wrap her in a towel and hold her close until her tears dried.

After what seemed like a long time, Maria lifted Sofia out of the water.

Grabbing a towel, Venom hurried forward and wrapped it around Sofia, gently drying her skin and the tears from her cheeks.

Maria handed her over to Venom and slipped the T-shirt over the child's head.

He carried her into the bedroom, laid her on the bed and sank into the chair beside her.

Working with a sick child was heart-wrenching. How did a parent know what to do and when?

He didn't know how to parent, but he had a whole new respect for those who raised healthy, happy boys and girls. It wasn't all fun and games.

Maria waited a few minutes and then measured Sofia's temperature.

Venom held his breath through the process.

When she looked up, his heart sank into his shoes. "No change?" he asked.

"None," Maria sighed. "Looks like we're going to the ER."

With his heart in his throat, Venom nodded, unable to speak, afraid he'd lied to the little girl with the promise that she would be all right. He was afraid their race across the country had taken its toll on this small, incredible little human.

And he was afraid she wouldn't make it because of a decision he'd made to drive up the western route.

The image of the little boy in the Afghan village surfaced like a bad omen, with Sofia's pretty face superimposed over that boy's dead body.

Venom shook himself hard.

*Oh, hell no. This child will not die.*

*Not if I can do anything about it.*

"Let's get her to the hospital." He wrapped her in a blanket, marched her out to the waiting SUV and sat in the seat behind the driver with Maria and Sofia.

After buckling the little girl in and securing his own belt, he reached for Maria's hand and held it all the way into Fool's Gold, through the pass and down into Colorado Springs.

Whatever happened, he and Maria would face it together. If he could do anything to help, he would.

The cartel threat took a backseat to Sofia's illness.

Venom hoped Diego and the cartel got that memo and laid off while Sofia recovered.

# CHAPTER 9

JoJo DROVE with Max in the front passenger seat of the SUV.

Maria's stomach twisted in a knot, and her heart ached all the way into Colorado Springs. Her dash for freedom from a terrible man had resulted in nearly losing her daughter to a landslide and getting her so sick she needed emergency medical attention. What kind of mother did that to her child?

Venom squeezed her hand gently. "She's tough. A fighter like her mother."

"But she's so small. Her body is so fragile," Maria whispered, her gaze on her daughter's face flushed with fever. She lay with her cheek across Venom's thigh, so still, her breath shallow, her chest barely moving.

Would they ever get there?

What seemed like an eternity passed before JoJo

pulled into the Emergency Room entrance at the Children's Hospital in Colorado Springs.

As soon as the vehicle came to a halt, Maria popped the buckle on her seatbelt and then Sofia's. Venom jumped out of the SUV and gently lifted Sofia into his arms.

Maria hurried around the vehicle and entered the hospital at his side.

The first hurdle was getting past the receptionist, who was taking names and insurance cards.

Maria hesitated to give a name and certainly had no medical insurance card or any other form of identification.

"I'm sorry, ma'am. We need some form of identification," the woman said. "We can't treat the child without it."

A second administrative person stepped up beside the woman who'd demanded Maria's ID. He leaned close and whispered what sounded like *let them in.*

The woman's eyes widened, and she looked up at the young man behind her. "*The* Sadie McClain? Wow." She turned to Maria. "You know Sadie McClain personally?"

Maria started to say no.

Before she could, Venom nudged her arm and spoke first. "My fiancée and I are close friends. I work for her husband. They take care of their people."

"I'll say they do," the woman said, clicking keys on her keyboard. "They pretty much gave us a blank check to cover all of your expenses." A printer whirred beside her. "All I need is a signature from one of the child's parents that allows us to treat her."

As Maria signed the paper, a nurse pushing a gurney stepped through the door marked Authorized Personnel Only.

"If you'll lay her on the bed, we'll get her right back to an exam room."

Venom laid Sofia on the gurney, blanket and all.

"Mommy?" Sofia called out.

"Right here, *mija*." Maria stepped up beside her daughter and took her hand. "This nice nurse is going to take you back to see the doctor."

Sofia's hot hand gripped hers. "Don't leave me."

"You can come with her," the nurse said. She stepped up to a large square button on the wall and pressed it.

The automatic door opened. She gripped the end of the gurney and pulled it through the wide opening.

Maria and Venom walked alongside the bed, within sight of Sofia.

"I'm scared," Sofia whispered, her gaze moving from Maria to Venom.

Maria's heart clenched. Sofia hadn't been in a hospital since she'd been born. It was a big, strange place with people she didn't know, and it smelled of disinfectant.

Maria squeezed her hand. "It's okay, *chica*. The

nice nurses and doctors are going to find out why you're sick. I'll be with you the whole time."

Her daughter turned to Venom. "And Mr. Vincent?"

"I'll be here, too," he answered with a smile.

The nurse led them down a hallway with rooms on either side. Some were occupied with patients and other nurses. She stopped at an empty room and turned the bed.

Maria and Venom stepped aside as the woman positioned the bed in the room and fluffed the pillow behind Sofia's head. "Is that better?"

Sofia nodded, her eyelids fluttering shut.

Her lashes lay against bluish-purple shadows beneath her eyes.

Maria worried that she'd fallen sick so fast.

The nurse turned to Maria and gave her half a smile. "Ma'am, could I speak to you alone?"

Maria frowned, her pulse quickening. Why alone? Was she afraid of saying something in front of Sofia? Something that might frighten the little girl?

She followed the nurse out of the room and down the hallway, out of earshot of Sofia and Venom.

The nurse leaned close, a frown pulling her brown low. "Do you want a doctor to look at that shiner?" she whispered. "Are you being held under duress by the man you came in with?"

Maria let go of the breath she hadn't realized she was holding and gave a short laugh. "No. No. You have it all wrong. That man helped me get away from the man who did this." She touched the bruised eye she hadn't thought about since before the landslide. She must have lost her sunglasses when they'd been bounced all over the place as they'd traveled down the hillside on a river of mud.

The nurse stared into her eyes, her frown deepening. "Are you sure? You don't have to cover for him. I can have security here in a heartbeat."

"I'm absolutely sure. Thank you for your concern. It's nice to know you're looking out for abuse victims." Maria touched the woman's arm. "But if anyone comes looking for my daughter or me, don't let them know we're here, and inform me immediately. The man who did this is dangerous."

The nurse's eyes widened. "That's good to know. I'll let the front desk know as well. I'll be back with the doctor." She left Maria and hurried back the way they'd come.

Maria entered the exam room and stepped beside Venom, slipping her hand into his. "I just want you to know how much I appreciate all you've done for me."

He stared down at her, his brow wrinkling. "What brought that on?"

"The nurse asked me if I wanted to see a doctor about my eye." Maria smiled. "She asked if I was being held under duress and if I wanted her to call security."

Venom cocked an eyebrow. "I'm glad she asked rather than jumping to conclusions."

"Me, too." She leaned into him. "I let her know

you were the one to get me away from the abuser. I told her that if anyone came looking for Sofia or me, not to share our location and let us know immediately."

"Good." He glanced out the open door. "Unfortunately, being in such a public place in Colorado Springs, we're somewhat exposed. Hopefully, the doctors can get Sofia on the mend soon so we can get you two somewhere safer."

Maria nodded. "First things first."

"That's right. Sofia's health is top priority." He squeezed her hand.

The doctor entered the room, introduced himself and questioned Maria about Sofia's symptoms.

She gave him a watered-down version of their previous night, only including the fact that they'd broken down on the road and had been forced to walk several miles in the rain.

He'd accepted her story without comment and turned his attention to Sofia, checking her heart, lungs, ears, nose and throat. He scheduled a blood draw, had a nurse start her on an anti-inflammatory and an IV, and told Maria to keep her hydrated while they waited for the results.

Sofia stayed awake and answered questions the doctor asked. She didn't cry when the phlebotomist stuck a needle in her arm and collected a blood sample.

Maria suspected she was too tired and a little fuzzy-headed with the effects of the high fever.

When the doctor and nurses left the room, Sofia held up her hand.

Maria was at her side instantly, wrapping her fingers around hers. "See? He's going to figure out why you're sick and make you feel better."

Her daughter held up her other hand, glancing bleary-eyed toward Venom.

He swung around the other side of the bed and took her hand in his. "Hey, kid."

"Hey," she responded and closed her eyes.

She slept while the adults stood guard, living up to their promises that they wouldn't leave her.

"I'm worried about leaving here," Maria whispered. "I don't want her to get worse."

"Hopefully, the doctor won't release Sofia until he's confident her fever is under control and she's on the path to recovery." He glanced across the bed at Maria and gave her a little smile that helped to reassure her.

Just having him there made Maria better capable of handling whatever diagnosis the doctor had to offer. She wasn't alone.

For a man she'd only just met, she trusted him not only with her life but with her baby's life. He might be harboring the effects of PTSD from his time in service, but he hadn't let that take his attention away from ensuring their safety.

He was strong, smart, loyal and kind to women and small children. Sofia had already fallen in love with him and trusted him when she had no reason to trust any man.

Maria could fall in love with Venom if she let herself. And it was hard to hold back when he was so ruggedly handsome that one soft glance from his gray eyes had her knees wobbling and her panties damp. And his kiss…

She glanced away, afraid he'd somehow see the direction of her thoughts or the desire simmering beneath the surface.

Yeah, they hadn't known each other long, but what they'd experienced together had formed a bond, at least on her side, that she couldn't dispel. Nor did she want to.

She worried that her judgment might've been skewed by the traumatic events. Once the danger passed, she might not react as strongly toward this man. Her gaze returned to him.

The concern he demonstrated toward her daughter, and the way he was gentle with her and her mother, were undeniable and compelling. He was one of those guys her mother would have called a "keeper." He'd make a great husband for some lucky woman and a terrific father who'd want to spend time with his kids, teaching them things his father had taught him.

She smiled at how he'd talked with Sofia while she'd been delirious with fever, talking about taking her fishing and teaching her how to swim.

Diego had never once offered to do anything with

Sofia. He hadn't even wanted to have his name on her birth certificate. He'd said that, because he was part of the cartel, he didn't want warring cartels to target her.

Maria suspected he hadn't wanted to be on the birth certificate in case she did manage to leave him and eventually sued for child support.

She was glad Diego's name wasn't on Sofia's birth certificate. He didn't deserve to be named as her father.

She was a kind, compassionate little girl who deserved a kind, compassionate father who would openly love and protect her from harm.

Someone like Venom.

After an hour of standing at Sofia's bedside, Maria was happy when the doctor returned.

A nurse accompanied him and took Sofia's vital signs.

"Good news is the fever is falling," the doctor said. "The blood test shows she has strep. She'll need to be on antibiotics until the prescription runs out. She'll need to take the full course, even if she feels better before you run out. If she stops halfway through, the infection could flare back up, and she could be back in the same condition she's in now."

"We'll make sure she sees the medication through to the end," Maria assured him.

"As long as her fever continues to fall, I see no reason to keep her overnight. She'll be much more comfortable in her own bed. She's already down to a relatively safe temperature. By the time we set up the discharge papers, you should be good to go."

"Thank you, doctor," Maria said, relief lightening the heaviness in her chest.

"Keep her warm and dry. It wouldn't hurt for her to stay in bed the rest of the day and maybe even tomorrow. Once the antibiotics kick in, she'll start feeling much better." The doctor turned to Sofia. "Do as your mother says, and you'll be fine." With a wink, he left the room.

Maria let go of a heartfelt sigh. "Strep. We can deal with that." She smiled at Sofia. "And we get to go home tonight."

Sofia's brow wrinkled, and she shook her head slowly. "Home?"

Maria's heart contracted. "Oh, *mija*. We're never going back to Diego's home. For now, home is wherever you and I are. The lodge where we slept last night is our home until we figure out where we'll go next."

Sofia's brow cleared. "I like that place."

Maria smiled. "Me, too."

The nurse came into the room, pushing a wheelchair and carrying Sofia's discharge instructions. All they needed to do was sign, pick up the prescription at the pharmacy on the corner outside the hospital and they could go home.

While Maria signed papers, Venom wrapped Sofia in the same blanket she'd arrived in and settled her into the wheelchair.

With her fever almost under control, Sofia was more awake and delighted to go for a ride in the wheelchair.

When they emerged into the lobby, JoJo and Max rose from chairs and hurried over.

"Sorry you had to wait so long," Maria said.

"Don't be. We ran a couple of errands before we came back here. We would've waited in the SUV, but I remembered neither of you has a cell phone." She grinned up at Max. "We had a chance to catch up on some home renovation shows. It gave us some ideas on what we want in the way of a home while keeping an eye out for any suspicious characters."

Maria hugged her friend. "You've done so much for us. Thank you."

JoJo stepped back and shrugged. "I'm just glad I could help. If you want to wait by the door, Max and I will bring the SUV around to pick you up." She ruffled Sofia's hair. "Glad you're feeling better."

Minutes later, they were all tucked into the vehicle. They picked up the medication at the pharmacy and headed west for Fool's Gold.

Thankfully, Diego's spies hadn't made a move. Hopefully, they still didn't know where exactly she was, giving her a little more time for Sofia to recover and for her to come up with a plan.

After their exposure to the public at the hospital, Maria knew it was only a matter of time before the cartel zeroed in on their location.

She and Sofia would need to find a secret location where no one would find them.

A selfish part of her wanted Venom to come with them.

She didn't dare to hope he could disappear with them, but it would be nice to have him around for a little longer.

Maria would like to have him around for a lot longer. What were the chances of that?

She wouldn't even try to guess.

Sofia lay across Venom's lap for the drive through the city. Once they started through the pass, she sat up, intrigued by the view of mountains rising on either side of her. Snow covered the highest peaks, making her clap her hands.

When they arrived at the Lodge, Gunny, RJ and Jake came out on the porch accompanied by a woman with sandy-blond hair and a friendly smile.

Venom carried Sofia up the steps to the porch.

"You're looking a little better than when you left." Gunny chucked her beneath her chin. "Are you hungry?"

She nodded. "Yes, sir."

"Good, because I made a big pot of mac-n-cheese." He frowned, touching a finger to his chin. "Oh, wait. Little girls don't eat mac-n-cheese, do they?"

Sofia nodded solemnly. "I do."

"Oh, good. I thought I'd have to throw out the

entire pot. But first, these ladies have something for you and your mama." He turned to RJ and the blonde.

RJ hooked the other woman's arm and dragged her forward. "This is Laurel Layne. She owns the flower shop in town. She's been busy, but I'll let her tell you." RJ stepped back.

Laurel's cheeks flushed a pretty pink. "I didn't do much. I just asked a few of my customers if they had any clothes they no longer needed that might fit a woman a little taller than me and a little shorter than RJ. I also asked if they had anything that might fit a five-year-old girl." She stepped aside to reveal two large, bulging kitchen garbage bags. "They came through. Now, none of the clothes are new, but they assured me they were clean. And there are several pairs of shoes of different sizes. Some of them look like they've never been worn.

"Oh, and this was nice." She reached into one of the bags and pulled out a cotton-candy pink teddy bear. "A customer came in about the time the ladies were delivering their items. When I told him we were collecting for a woman and a child who'd lost every-thing, he went down to the gift shop, bought this teddy bear and brought it back as his contribution." She held out the bear to Sofia. "Would you like this pink teddy bear?"

Sofia looked to Maria for permission.

"You can have it," Maria said.

Sofia took the stuffed animal from Laurel and pressed her face against its fake fur.

"We can get the guys to carry these up to your room," RJ said. "I hope you can use the items. But if you aren't comfortable wearing used clothing, Again, no worries."

Maria covered her mouth with her hand, staring at the bulging bags, her heart swelling so much it might burst from her chest. "Please, tell your customers thank you from the bottom of my heart. I've never had anyone treat me so nicely. I hope one day to be able to repay you for your kindness."

"You don't owe us anything," RJ insisted. "We're just women looking out for each other."

Max grabbed one of the bags. Jake took the other. They headed up the stairs.

RJ turned to Maria. "Go. See if anything fits. I'm sure you'd like to get out of what you're wearing and into something that isn't splattered with mud."

Maria looked down at the only clothes she had since leaving Diego and the cartel. They were stiff from being wet, doused with mud and then dried while she'd been on the run. Her white tennis shoes were ruined. Stained from slogging through the mud, they'd never be white again, but it wouldn't hurt to clean them. They still had a lot of wear left in them.

RJ had the men drop both bags in Maria's room. Venom carried Sofia in and laid her on the bed. When she smiled up at him, Maria's heart warmed.

He bent to press a kiss on Sofia's forehead. "Remember, you're supposed to be recovering. Don't get too rambunctious."

Her brow twisted. "I don't know what that is."

"No running around and getting all excited," Maria offered. "You need to rest so that you don't start feeling bad again."

Sofia nodded and lay back against the pillow.

RJ and Laurel entered after the men left and dumped the contents of the bags on the end of the bed.

Sofia sat forward and sifted through the girl's clothes, exclaiming over the shirt with the Little Mermaid on it and the pink leggings with white bows printed all over them. When she found a matching pink shirt, she hugged them to her. "Can I wear these?" she asked.

"You can wear anything you like," Laurel said with a smile. "They're yours."

Sofia clapped her hands and then tried to pull JoJo's loaner T-shirt over her head.

"Let me help," JoJo said and dragged the shirt over Sofia's head and helped her into the pink shirt with the white bows. Then she helped her into the leggings. By the time she was fully dressed, she laid back on the pillow, tired from that little bit of effort. However, the smile on her face was priceless.

While JoJo had been helping Sofia, RJ and Laurel sifted through the clothes that were more Maria's size.

Laurel pulled out a pair of jeans and held them up to Maria. "These might fit."

RJ found a rib-knit sweater in a soft gray that

matched the color of Venom's eyes. "This will be nice. And there's a denim jacket as well." She held up the jacket.

Between the four women, they sorted through the clothes, setting aside the items obviously too small for Maria and Sofia and stuffed them into one of the plastic bags. Then they added the items too big for Maria to the bag but set aside the clothes too big for Sofia.

"She'll eventually grow into those," Maria said.

Maria tried on the shoes that had been sent, finding a pair of sneakers that were a close fit and a pair of cowboy boots that fit like they'd been made for her. She walked across the room in them, grinning. "I've never owned a pair of cowboy boots."

"Well, now you do." RJ crossed her arms over her chest. "I'll bet you've never been on a horse, either."

Maria shook her head. "Never."

"We'll have to do something about that, won't we, ladies?" RJ looked at JoJo and Laurel. Each nodded.

Maria's smile faded. "I don't know that I'll be around long enough to learn to ride."

RJ frowned. "We'll have to see about that as well."

Maria didn't try to change their minds. To keep Sofia safe from Diego and the cartel, she'd have to leave, change their identities and start all new lives in a place no one knew them.

The thought took some of the happiness out of the excitement of new-to-her clothes.

Laurel's eyes rounded. "Oh, one more thing. I left

it in my car." She ran out of the room and down the stairs.

Maria, RJ and JoJo folded the items to be kept and stacked them on a chair. By the time they'd finished, Laurel was back with a huge shopping bag from a local department store. She handed it to Maria. "This is from us. Some things you don't want second-hand."

Maria set the bag on the end of the bed and pulled each item out, one at a time.

"It's a kind of care package," Laurel explained.

There was a package of panties, enough for each day of the week for Maria and Sofia, a package of toothbrushes and toothpaste, shampoo, conditioner, ponytail holders, socks, hand lotion, mascara, a tube of lipstick, two hairbrushes, a comb, a curling iron and a blow dryer. There were even two pairs of sunglasses and two baseball caps.

Tears welled in her eyes and spilled down her cheeks. She swallowed hard on the lump lodged in her throat. "I don't…know how to thank you."

JoJo hugged her. "Then don't. We've all been through hard times."

Laurel nodded. "All of us." She added herself to the hug.

RJ joined them. "That's why we stick together and pay it forward." She was first to take a step back. She brushed a hand across her eyes.

Laurel laughed and wiped away tears of her own. "Look at us, boohooing like a bunch of girly-girls."

She shooed the other two women toward the door. "Let Maria change into something pretty for dinner. We're all staying for mac-n-cheese." She winked at Sofia. "We're all starving, so don't be too long."

The women left, pulling the door closed behind them.

The sudden silence was almost depressing.

For the first time in over five years, Maria had been surrounded by women who could be her friends.

Too bad she wouldn't be staying long.

# CHAPTER 10

MARIA SMOOTHED a hand over Sofia's hair.

Her daughter stared up at her. "I like them."

Sudden tears welled in Maria's eyes. "Me, too." She refused to cry. Her job as a mother was to be strong for her daughter. Maria squared her shoulders, scooped all the toiletries back into the bag and carried them into the bathroom.

She returned to the stack of clothes, wondering what would look best on her. If she looked good, she would feel good. Or so she told herself. The truth was, she wanted to show Venom she didn't always resemble a drowned sewer rat. She could clean up nicely when she had sufficient motivation.

Making Venom look twice was sufficient motivation. After careful consideration, she selected a slim-fitting camel-colored skirt and a cream sweater that would contrast nicely with her light brown skin and black hair.

With the clothing in one hand, she entered the bathroom, leaving the door ajar so that she could listen in case Sofia needed her.

Maria stripped out of the clothes she'd worn through her escape from El Paso and the landslide that had nearly killed them and dropped them in a pile on the floor. She wanted to burn them as part of putting her past behind her. However, considering she didn't have much, she figured she needed everything she had. Especially if she was going back to work.

Though she didn't want to take too much time getting ready, she still wanted to rinse off after removing the dirty clothes she'd worn that day and the day before. She turned on the water in the shower. Then she piled her hair on top of her head and secured it in a loose bun with one of the new ponytail holders. After adjusting the temperature, she stepped beneath the spray and used some of the body wash that had been included in the care package. It had a pleasing scent that reminded her of citrus and honeysuckle.

She lathered and rinsed, splashing water on her face, careful not to get her hair too wet. She'd washed it the night before. As thick as it was, it took a long time to dry.

Out of the shower, she turned off the water, dried her body and used the brush to smooth the tangles. Then she secured it in a neat ponytail at the nape of her neck.

A smooth layer of lotion softened her skin and made her feel good all over. Next on was one of the pairs of panties. She tore open the pack only to discover they were thong panties. She'd never worn thong panties and wasn't sure she'd like them.

With no other option, she slid her legs into a pair and pulled them up.

Not bad.

They made her feel naughty and sexy all under. A smile tugged at her lips as she wondered what Venom would think of the little scraps of fabric that left her butt cheeks completely bare.

Her little secret would be hers alone.

Fortunately, the sports bra was made of a thin fabric that laid flat against her body. It was a little snug over her breasts but good enough. Next, she drew the sweater over her head and smoothed it over her chest and waist. It was a soft cashmere that hugged her figure perfectly. The skirt fit as well, the hem reaching just below her knees.

As she stepped out of the bathroom, she remembered, she didn't have any dressy shoes to wear with the outfit. The sneakers were too casual, and her original shoes were too dirty and casual as well. Which left the boots.

She pulled on a pair of socks and then the boots and stood.

"Mommy, you're so pretty," Sofia said from where she lay on the bed.

"Thank you, *chica*." She ducked into the bathroom

for a brush and came back out to her daughter. "Are you hungry?" she asked as she ran the brush through Sofia's hair, which was so very much like her own.

Sofia nodded and winced when Maria caught a hidden snarl.

"Sorry," Maria said and took a little more time, working through the tangles until Sofia's hair lay soft and straight over her shoulders. "Do you want a braid or a ponytail?"

"I want a ponytail like yours." Sofia sat on the edge of the bed, patiently waiting for Maria to finish.

"I think I saw a pair of pink sneakers and a white sweater among the things they brought." Maria looked around the room and found several pairs of shoes in a row. She brought the pink sneakers over, along with a pair of socks from the care package.

Sofia pulled on the socks and shoes and slid off the bed onto her feet.

Maria pressed her fingers against the toes of the shoes. "Just a little big. That gives you room to grow." She straightened and helped her daughter into the cardigan.

"There," she said. "We both look great." Her brow dipped. "Are you sure you're up to sitting at the dinner table? I could bring a bowl of mac-n-cheese up to you."

Sofia slipped her hand into Maria's. "I want to sit with everyone. They're so nice." Her gaze grew solemn. "When we leave, I won't see them ever again. That makes me sad."

"I know," Maria said. "It makes me sad, too. We could have all been friends."

Sofia looked up. "Will we have new friends where we go next?"

Maria's heart squeezed hard in her chest. "We will, *chica*. We'll have lots of friends." She hoped that was true.

They stepped through the door and turned, almost running into Venom.

Maria blinked. "Oh. There you are."

He pushed away from the wall he'd been leaning on and offered her his arm. "Just waiting on my girls so that we can go down to dinner together."

"Sorry we took so long," Maria said.

"I'm not," he said with a grin. "You're both beautiful."

Sofia hit him with a full-faced grin. "Aren't we? And Mommy has boots." She pointed to Maria's feet.

Heat rushed into her cheeks. "It was boots or sneakers."

"You made the right choice." His gaze swept her from head to toe. "The whole outfit looks like designer couture."

Maria laughed. "What do you know about designer couture?"

He grinned. "Absolutely nothing. But that fact doesn't diminish my appetite for mac-n-cheese in the least." He held out his arm. "Shall we?"

"Yes, we should." She hooked her arm through his

and let him guide her down the stairs to the dining room.

A few guests were scattered around the individual tables, eating their meals and talking quietly among themselves.

The long table near the kitchen had been set with plates, cutlery, napkins and glasses of ice. The lodge staff and Brotherhood Protectors usually sat at this table.

At that moment, the table was unoccupied.

Voices sounded from the kitchen.

Gunny burst through the door carrying a tray with a huge ham. He set it in the middle of the table. "Grab a seat. The others are in the kitchen to help bring out the rest of the meal."

One by one, people emerged bearing entrees.

First, after Gunny was RJ, her hands covered in oven mitts, carrying a steaming broccoli casserole. She was followed by Max, with a pitcher of tea in one hand and a pitcher of lemonade in the other. JoJo sailed through with a basket of bread rolls. Laurel followed with a colorful salad and a couple of bottles of dressing.

Jake backed through the swinging door with a big bowl full of northern beans.

Though scents filled the air, making Maria's tummy rumble, she frowned. There was one person missing.

Venom flung open the swinging door. "Bet you

thought we'd forgotten the mac-n-cheese." He winked at Sofia.

She giggled. "I did think someone forgot."

"I think we're all looking forward to Gunny's mac-n-cheese," JoJo said. "It's the best."

As they settled around the table, Maria sat beside Sofia, with JoJo on the other side of Sofia. Venom set the casserole dish of mac-n-cheese in front of them and claimed the seat on the other side of Maria.

Conversation was lively as they passed bowls and platters around, filling them with the delicious food Gunny and RJ had prepared.

Sofia not only ate the mac-n-cheese, she managed a small slice of ham, a couple of bites of the cheesy broccoli casserole, half a bread roll and a cup of lemonade.

Maria caught up with JoJo since she'd left the service, but throughout the meal, her focus was off.

Or rather, it was on the thigh brushing against hers—warm, muscular and Venom's.

Her heartbeat couldn't settle into a steady beat the entire meal.

He'd changed into khaki slacks and a black pullover sweater that complimented his sandy-blond hair and gray eyes.

She wanted to reach over and lay her hand on his thigh, to feel the ripple of his muscles every time he moved.

A spark of joy nestled deep inside. For the past five years, she'd believed she was passionless and unable to experience an orgasm. Diego had fed that belief each time he'd forced her to have sex with him.

Just touching her thigh to Venom's had her entire body burning with desire. All he would have to do was touch her in the right place, and she'd come apart.

Which proved to Maria she wasn't passionless. Sitting beside Venom, her body was burning with passion.

The problem had been Diego. His abuse had killed any love or passion she might have felt for the man.

THE LONGER DINNER LASTED, the more Venom wanted to rip off his shirt and pound his chest. Well, maybe he didn't really want to go all male gorilla on the woman next to him, but he was so hard he doubted he could stand at the moment. When Maria had stepped out of her room wearing that sweater that clung to every luscious curve of her breasts, with the skirt accentuating the swell of her hips, his blood had gone primal, pounding through his veins to the beat of an ancient drum.

He would have been more at ease had he sat across the table from her. Beside her, his thigh touched hers every time he moved. If he were honest with himself, he moved a lot...on purpose, just to connect to her and feel her warmth.

Here, they were surrounded by people, and all

Venom could think about was getting naked with Maria.

If people could read minds...he'd be in deep shit.

The woman was his client. She'd been abused for years and didn't need a horny ex-SEAL panting after her. She had enough problems with a sick kid and an ex-boyfriend breathing down her neck.

When Sofia leaned against Maria and laid her head on her mother's lap, it was the excuse he'd been waiting for.

He rose and stepped around to the other side of Maria. "Come on, Sofia. I'll take you up to bed. You should be resting after the day you've had."

She raised her arms for him to pick her up. As she laid her head on his shoulder, she said, "Gunny made mac-n-cheese."

The adults around the table chuckled.

"Well, you got Gunny's mac-n-cheese," JoJo said. "But you don't have to stay up with the rest of us." She smiled up at Sofia.

"I'll go with you." Maria pushed back in her chair and stood.

"You don't have to leave the table," he said half-heartedly, when he really wanted her to come with them. "I'm sure Sofia and I can figure out how to tuck her in."

Maria smiled, sending a shaft of desire straight to his core. "It's okay. It's been a stressful couple of days. I'm as tired as she is." She turned to the people at the table. "Thank you all for taking us in and seeing to all our needs. I really don't know what I would've done if I hadn't called JoJo." She pressed a hand to her friend's shoulder. "Thank you. And thank you for a wonderful dinner with such good company. You're all so fortunate to have each other. Good night."

A chorus of goodnights followed them as Venom led the way out of the dining room and up the stairs to the bedroom Maria and her daughter shared.

He entered and laid Sofia on the bed. Then he bent, kissed her forehead and tucked the pink teddy bear in next to the girl. "You two sleep tight."

Sofia tucked the bear under her arm and closed her eyes.

When Venom straightened, he caught Maria looking at him, her hand pressed to her breast, her dark eyes smoldering.

Or was that wishful thinking on his part?

He wanted her passion as smoldering hot as his was.

Maria blinked and turned away.

Hell, even if she wanted to make love with him, they couldn't very well do it with Sofia in the room.

He was destined to take a cold shower and go to bed alone in the room on the other side of the wall from her.

As Venom strode past Maria, she turned and touched his arm.

He stopped. His breath arrested in his lungs. When he raised his gaze to meet hers, there was no mistaking it.

Her eyes were smoldering.

"Do you feel it?" she whispered.

He leaned his head back and groaned. "By *feel it*, do you mean is my heart working overtime, pumping blood through my veins so fast it heats every inch of my body like a percolating volcano?"

She nodded. Her fingers curled into the sleeve of his black sweater.

*Holy hell.*

"It's taking every ounce of my control to keep from kissing you," he said through gritted teeth.

Her eyes flared. "What if I want you to kiss me?"

He drew a deep breath, held it a moment and let it out slowly. "Sweetheart, if I start kissing you, I don't think I could stop."

Her breasts rose and fell in that figure-hugging sweater, tempting him beyond salvation.

"Mommy?" Sofia called out, cutting through the growing tension between the adults.

Venom met Maria's gaze. "Your daughter needs you, and I need to go." He brushed past her and jerked open the door. As he paused on the threshold, he turned back. "If you need me, all you have to do is yell. Until then, lock the door."

He stepped out into the hallway and pulled the door closed behind him. For a long moment, he stood there, counting his breaths and willing his body to relax.

He didn't leave his post until a solid click indicated she'd locked the deadbolt. And still, he remained standing there, fighting an internal battle between what he wanted and what he knew was the right thing to do.

The locked door would keep out an intruder and it would keep him from marching through it, dragging her into his arms and crushing her mouth with his.

He laid his hand on the door, so close to knocking and asking her to let him back in.

What would that change? She wasn't alone. He was supposed to protect her, not molest her.

Venom leaned his forehead against the cool door panel for a moment. Then he stepped away and entered his room, closing the door with a soft click.

He stripped out of his nice clothes and stood in his boxer briefs, letting the cool air carry some of the heat away from his body.

It wasn't enough.

For the next half hour, he paced the floor, listening for any noise coming from their room. The pacing was ridiculous and served no other purpose but to allow him time to relax his tight groin and for his pulse to slow to a normal rate.

Finally, he lay on the bed, on top of the overs, staring up at the ceiling. The only light penetrating the darkness was that of the stars shining through the window.

Though he closed his eyes, sleep did not come. He checked the clock on the nightstand every hour, willing the night to pass so he could get up and start another day. Sleep wasn't going to happen. Not with his thoughts on the woman in the next room and how wrong it would be to take advantage of her when she was just getting out of a bad situation.

She might be feeling something for him, but what if her desire was grounded in gratitude for his help? He didn't want gratitude. He wanted more. And he couldn't ask it of her.

She needed time to regroup to remember who she was as an individual and love herself before she loved someone else. At least that was the psycho-babble advice given to those people ending abusive relationships and starting over.

Every time he heard a noise, he sat up and pressed his ear to the wall. Not a sound emanated from the other side. He wished Maria snored. Then at least he'd know she was there, sleeping peacefully.

Just past midnight, a floorboard squeaked outside his bedroom door.

Venom was out of the bed in a second. He grabbed the Glock on his way across the room and had his hand on the doorknob when someone knocked.

He jumped, not expecting a knock from someone creeping around the lodge.

"Venom," a deep voice called out. "It's Jake."

He flipped the deadbolt and opened the door to find Jake standing there, still dressed in the clothes he'd worn at dinner. A frown deepened the lines on his forehead.

Venom tensed. "What's wrong?"

"RJ heard some customers talking in Gunny's Watering Hole tonight, which leads us to think the cartel has found us."

Venom's pulse sped. "What did she hear?"

"A couple of men were asking if anyone had seen a Hispanic woman and her five-year-old daughter around who weren't from the area. They said they were looking because she'd kidnapped the girl, and the child's parents were desperate to get her back."

"Bastard," Venom bit out. "It's time to move them."

"Agreed," Jake said. "I've called in a few members of our team. They'll be here in fifteen minutes. I don't know if those men know Maria and Sofia are here at the lodge, but we're going to assume they're watching and move accordingly."

Venom nodded. "We're taking them to the safe house, right?"

"Yes, but we're not all going there. When everyone gets here, we'll go over the plan. In the meantime, we need to get Maria and Sofia ready to go."

Venom gave him a curt nod.

"We'll meet in the war room in fifteen." Jake turned and walked away.

The door beside his cracked open, and Maria peered out. "Venom, what's going on?"

His jaw tight, the Glock still in his hand, he said, "Get dressed and pack what you need. We move tonight."

# CHAPTER 11

JAKE, dressed in black, stood at the end of the conference table, pointing to the map image projected on the wall behind him. "We'll load three look-alike vehicles with Maria and Sofia—at least they'll all appear to be Maria and Sofia. Each driver will have someone riding shotgun in case the cartel opens fire."

Max sat at Jake's right. Three other team members were scattered around the table, having introduced themselves as Sawyer, Weaver and Tayo. All the men, including Venom, wore black pants, long-sleeved black shirts and black boots.

"I'll ride with Venom, Maria and the child, team Whiskey," Jake said. "Max with Sawyer will take JoJo, Team Tango. Weaver with Tayo will have RJ with them, Team Foxtrot."

Sawyer chuckled. "Whiskey, Tango, Foxtrot."

At Maria's confused frown, Venom leaned toward her and explained. "The acronym for *What The Fuck*."

"Cute." RJ, her lips twisted in a wry grin, appeared with a stack of dark ball caps and gave one to each man.

JoJo tossed three dark gray, zip-up hoodie jackets onto the table, three olive green woolen Army blankets and two king-size pillows. "I know the jackets are big, but they'll disguise the different shapes of our bodies, and the hoods will shroud our facial features."

RJ grabbed a blanket and wrapped it around a pillow. "JoJo and I will carry pillows wrapped in blankets as decoys for Sofia. Maria will have her daughter wrapped in a similar blanket. We'll get into the three vehicles simultaneously."

RJ and JoJo slid their arms into the oversized hoodies, pulled the hoods over their heads and around their faces, hiding their features from anyone who might be looking.

JoJo helped Maria into hers as she sat with a sleeping Sofia in her lap.

Jake continued, "Once everyone is in position, all three SUVs will head to town. When we get to Fool's Gold, we'll split up in three different directions. The goal is to split them up as well. Hopefully, they'll follow the wrong vehicles. If they end up following the one Maria and Sofia are in, we'll do our best to lose them before we take them to the safe house."

Jake picked up a cap, adjusted it to fit his head and pulled it down over his forehead, shadowing his features. While the other men followed suit, Jake leaned his fists on the table.

"We don't know how many are out there, if they're watching the lodge as we speak or when they'll make a move. We're going to try to make our move first." Jake straightened. "Hank will be here tomorrow. There's more to the cartel's story than trying to get Maria and Sofia back. He's coming to fill us in. Any questions?"

The men selected their preferred weapons and ammunition, body armor and radio headsets.

Jake and Max fitted the women with radios and body armor beneath their hoodies and performed a comm check among everyone in the room.

Venom held Sofia while Maria was outfitted. Her brow was dented in what appeared to be a perpetual frown. When she came to him to take Sofia, he bent and kissed her forehead. "You're going to be all right."

She shook her head. "How do you do it? This body armor is heavy. Between it and Sofia, I might not make it to the vehicle. And you have me decked out in body armor, but what about Sofia?"

"She couldn't carry it. We're banking on them not shooting at you and the other women for fear of hitting Sofia." He grimaced. "It's not much of an assurance, but why else would he go to so much trouble to follow you if he didn't plan on bringing you and Sofia back with him?"

"He might get tired of the chase and say fuck it and shoot us for all the trouble." Maria snorted. "I learned early on that he doesn't really care about us. We're possessions, and it pisses him off when someone takes his possessions."

Venom cupped her cheek. "You're so much more than possessions. He's a fool if he doesn't see that."

"He's a fool, all right," Maria said as she readjusted the hoodie over the body armor and her face. Then she reached for Sofia, wrapped in the green Army blanket and tucked her legs into the blanket to give her the same shape as the pillows RJ and JoJo were using as decoys.

Jake headed for the staircase. "As soon as we come out of the basement, we're all the same. No one should be able to tell one of the men from the other. No one should be able to identify the real Maria and Sofia."

RJ hefted her pillow beneath the blanket one last time and followed Jake up the stairs.

They moved through the kitchen in silence.

The pairs of men sandwiched their *Marias* and *Sofias* between them and escorted them out to their assigned vehicles.

Once they were all aboard, the SUVs left the lodge and drove out of Lost Valley Ranch onto the road leading into Fool's Gold. When they reached Main Street, Max with Sawyer and JoJo headed east. Weaver with Tayo and RJ hung a left toward the west, and Venom with Jake, Maria and Sofia went straight north.

Each vehicle would zigzag through Fool's Gold's

streets to shake any tails and then head out in their perspective directions, leading any residual hangers-on away from the others.

Jake drove while Venom rode shotgun, sitting at the edge of his seat, his head craning in all directions, searching for headlights or vehicles following with lights out.

For a short while, he thought he saw a dark sedan a couple of blocks back. Eventually, it pulled into an apartment complex.

"Any takers?" Jake asked into the headset.

"Team Foxtrot had one for a while but lost him near the casino," Tayo reported.

"It's quiet behind Team Tango," came Max's voice. "We're halfway to our turnaround."

"Nothing behind Team Whiskey," Venom said.

"It's quiet out here," Tayo said. "Even at the casino."

"Too quiet," Max agreed.

"Could be the cartel was just testing the waters and hasn't actually pinpointed the location of their target," Jake suggested. "If that's the case, we made the right decision to move them when we did. We'll head for the safe house, doing a few switchbacks on the way. When you get to your outer limit, turn around and head home."

"Team Tango, roger. We'll keep comm lines open."

"Team Foxtrot, roger. Comm lines open. See you back at headquarters."

The radio went silent as Jake drove backroads,

seeming to know all the cutoffs and through roads in the area and determined to use them all before he finally followed what appeared to be an abandoned rutted road up the side of a mountain, twisting back into a high valley.

In a clearing stood several weathered buildings, their windows dark maws sans the glass that held out the weather a century ago.

"It's a ghost town," Maria leaned forward, staring at the structures in front of them.

Jake nodded, a smile playing on his lips. "To anyone walking or driving up to it, that's exactly what it is. Now, watch this," he held up a remote-control device and pressed a button.

One of the old houses rose on struts, straight up in the air, revealing a modern staircase leading down into the ground, freshly painted with handrails and lighting.

"Hank bought the property from an old prospector who knew the history of this little ghost town. The original miners built the houses on top of their mine tunnels to hide the entrances from claim jumpers. They created a fake mine entrance further up the side of the mountain.

"Hank brought in engineers and construction workers from other states, who were prior military with top-secret clearances, had them sign non-disclosure agreements and put them to work enlarging the first landing-level below the buildings, reinforcing the tunnels, ceilings and walls and outfitting it to serve as living quarters with bedrooms, bathrooms and a kitchen. He's created other safe houses that could be used for fallout shelters as well in Montana, Wyoming, Washington and Idaho."

"Is Hank a prepper?" Maria asked. "Does he expect a nuclear holocaust sometime soon?"

Jake laughed. "No. But he has created spaces that could serve as fallout shelters, but mostly as safehouses for people where the federal witness protection program has failed them. He considers them temporary shelter until a permanent solution is arranged." Jake shifted into park and climbed down from the SUV.

Venom got out and lifted Sofia into his arms.

"Were you able to stow the bag I packed?" Maria asked as she slid out of the SUV onto the ground.

Venom nodded. "It's under the seat."

Maria reached for the gym bag containing a couple of changes of clothing for her and Sofia, along with the toiletries the women had provided.

Jake led them down the stairs into what had once been a mine shaft but was now a bright, open space with high ceilings and comfortable furnishings with artwork hanging on the walls that gave the appearance of windows overlooking sunlit Grecian gardens, Tuscan vineyards and white, sandy beaches.

Jake handed Maria the remote control. "Once you're inside, click the button and the abandoned building lowers, hiding the staircase.

"What's the power source?" Venom asked.

"Wind and solar, with power stored in battery units further back in the tunnels. There are propane-powered backup generators as well. You'll notice battery-powered lanterns positioned throughout the living spaces should you have a power outage. And there's a manual escape hatch that leads into the back of one of the old buildings."

"Show me," Maria said.

Jake led them to what appeared to be the pantry that had been fully stocked with enough staple items to see them through the apocalypse. He pulled a shelf full of paper products toward him, exposing a doorway and a set of stairs. "This leads up to the last old house in the row. When you reach the top of the stairs, you have to push a trap door up to get out. The door is on hydraulic hinges and is easy enough to manage on your own."

Venom was impressed with the amount of thought that had gone into setting up the safe house. The fact it was off the grid and could be self-sustaining when needed made it even more impressive.

Jake returned to the main living area, crossed to a door against the wall and pulled it open. "The ghost town is rigged with hidden cameras. You can monitor what's going on outside in this computer room. It's even connected to the internet via satellite. You can keep in touch with us via video and voice. The dish is camouflaged as an old cast iron pot like they used for everything from making lye to cleaning laundry."

Maria stood in the middle of the living room, her arms wrapped around her middle. "How long do you think we'll have to be down here?"

"Like I said, Hank's on his way here with some news he's learned from his contacts with the DEA." Jake planted his hands on his hips. "Hopefully, he'll have a better idea of where you'll be going next. In the meantime, you should be safe here."

Jake met Venom's gaze. "Swede also has access to the outside cameras and will be monitoring them as well. I'll be out every day to check on you. I'll come via a four-wheeler or side-by-side utility vehicle. If you need me to bring anything, text me."

Jake climbed the stairs up to the main entrance. Once he'd cleared the decoy ghost town building, Venom took the remote from Maria and closed the hatch, sealing them into the safe house.

"Where do you want Sofia to sleep?" he asked, still carrying the little girl, who'd only blinked her eyes open once the entire time he'd been holding her.

Maria looked around the living area as if lost. "I don't know," she said, rubbing her hands over her arms. "I appreciate that this place is safe..." She shook her head slowly, side to side. "But I don't like it." Her gaze shifted to him and locked as if clinging to a lifeline. "I didn't leave one prison to end up in another. This one doesn't even have windows or natural light."

Venom closed the distance between them. "We won't stay long. Just until Hank gets here and lets us know what's going on."

Maria nodded. "I know. I need to be flexible. I mean, beggars can't be choosers and all, but I'm not cut out to live in a cave. I'm from El Paso, where it's sunny three hundred and sixty-five days a year."

He rubbed his hand over her arm. "Let's get Sofia tucked into bed so she can sleep and recuperate. Then you and I can talk."

She reached for him. "I don't mean to be ungrateful."

He smiled. "I'm not judging you. I get it. We're in an enclosed cave. As spacious as it is, it's not open to the outside. Tell you what—we can monitor the surrounding area via the cameras. If the coast is clear, we'll get outside every day for sunlight and vitamin D."

She nodded. "Sounds good. And you're right. Sofia needs a proper bed to sleep in." Maria squared her shoulders and surveyed the bedrooms. Each was equipped with either a queen-sized or king-sized bed. One room had two queens. Another had a queen on one side of the room and a set of bunk beds on the other. In total, the safe house could easily accommodate a dozen or more people.

Maria selected the bedroom next to what she considered the master suite with the king-sized bed. The room beside it had a queen bed neatly made up with fresh sheets, a white down comforter and a teal fleece throw. Maria pulled the covers back and stepped aside as Venom laid Sofia on the mattress, her head resting on the pillow.

He tucked the blanket under Sofia's chin and brushed a kiss across her forehead. When he turned around, Maria had left the room.

She returned with the pink teddy bear a moment later and placed it beside her daughter. She kissed her cheek and straightened. "Do you think they have any wine in here?"

"They have everything else. Why don't you look for the wine? I want to explore a little more before we call it a night."

While Maria rummaged in the pantry and another storeroom recessed into the wall beyond the kitchen, Venom checked out the living room. A television was mounted against the wall. He located the remote and flipped through the streaming options, landing on a video of a flickering fireplace. It was nice, but it needed something else.

In a cabinet in one of the bedrooms, he located a space heater and carried it out into the living room, plugging it into a wall near the long white sectional. With the fireplace crackling cheerfully on the screen and the space heater providing warmth, it almost felt like the real fireplace at the lodge.

Maria came out of the storeroom with a bottle of red wine, two wine glasses and a corkscrew. "I hit pay dirt. There's an entire wine cellar in the very back of the storeroom."

She placed the bottle on the coffee table and handed him the corkscrew.

He opened the bottle and poured a healthy portion into each glass, then handed her one.

"What shall we toast to?" she asked. "Prison escapes, surviving an attack by Mother Nature, or going underground to avoid ex-boyfriends?"

He held up his glass. "How about toasting the amazing courage it took to get you this far?"

"Or the strength, intelligence and incredible patience a certain hero has demonstrated with a difficult client and her adorable daughter?"

"I'll go for all the above," Venom said. "As long as I get to drink the wine."

"Done." She touched her glass to his, and they drank.

Maria stared at the fake fire, her eyes narrowing. "This isn't quite right."

"Do you want a different kind of fire?" He held up the remote.

She shook her head. "No. That's not the problem." Maria took the glass from his hand and set hers and his on an end table along with the bottle of wine. "Help me move the coffee table."

He stood. "She hasn't been here a full hour, and she's already rearranging the furniture."

She rolled her eyes, bent and gripped one end of the coffee table. "Shut up and lift."

He did as he was told and lifted his end as she lifted hers. "Where are we going with it?"

"Moving it out of the way. Four feet over should be enough."

They placed it at the far end of the sectional, reclaimed their wine glasses and sat on the shag rug instead of the sofa.

Maria sighed. "Better."

"The only thing that could make it better is if it was a real fire," Venom said.

"I don't know. This isn't bad. There's no smoke, and neither one of us risks burning our fingers. Oh, and we don't have to put down our wine to add more wood." She lifted the glass.

He tapped his against hers. "I'll drink to that." Leaning back against the sofa, his shoulder touched hers.

She didn't move away.

He didn't move away.

His pulse quickened. Everything was ripe for the one thing they shouldn't do. If he were a gentleman and a professional protector, he'd set down his wine glass, get off his ass and march his butt to bed.

He leaned over and laid his glass on the table, fully intending to stop the insanity before it started.

But who was he kidding?

He only set down his glass to free his hands. Not to wave good night as he trotted off to bed. He'd free his hand so he could hold her while he kissed her like they were the last two humans on earth, and they only had hours to live in their post-apocalyptic bunker.

Maria handed her glass to him.

He set it next to his.

Before he dared to touch her, he'd give her a chance to stop him before he started. "I want to kiss you, Maria Elena. But I know that once I start, it'll be impossible to stop with just one kiss. It's your call. Just say no, and I'll walk away."

# CHAPTER 12

MARIA SHOOK HER HEAD SLOWLY, her heartbeat anything but slow.

Erratic. Yes. Slow. No.

His brow dipped. "You're shaking your head. Is that a no?"

"I'm not saying no," she said and laughed nervously. "Nothing like a double-negative to create confusion. I guess I should be clear, concise and leave no doubt as to my answer." What the hell was she doing? She leaned her head against his chest. "I'm botching this, and we still haven't kissed." Her head came up. "Can I start over?"

He chuckled. "Absolutely. Would you like another sip of wine first?"

She shook her head. "No. I want to be clear-headed and deliberate." Maria cupped his cheeks in her palms and brought her face close to his. "Yes. I want you to kiss me. No. I don't want you to stop there. And yes, I'm going to kiss you first."

She lowered her mouth to his, and all clear thought flew out the window.

Only there were no windows in the safe house. But they were safe. Sofia was asleep. They were two consenting adults with a fire burning, a shag rug beneath them and too many clothes between them.

What she started as a tentative exploration of his mouth changed when he caught the back of her head and brought her closer.

He crushed her lips and then swept past her teeth to claim her tongue in a sensuous caress that left her breathless and hungry for more.

Maria's pulse raced, and her breath grew ragged. The more he kissed her, the more naked she wanted to be.

His hands roamed over her back and downward to snag the hem of the gray sweater she'd worn in honor of the color of his eyes. The sweater came up over her head to be tossed across the floor.

Not to be outdone, she ran her hands down his torso and tugged his black sweater out of the waistband of his jeans. Then she pushed it up over his broad chest.

Venom leaned up and finished the job, his sweater joining hers on the floor.

Maria lost track of who was undressing whom as fingers fumbled, garments disappeared and they lay naked on the shag rug, panting and laughing softly.

She pushed up, leaning over his chest, loving being skin-to-skin. "I never knew making love could be funny," she whispered against the pulse beating erratically at the base of his throat.

"It can be anything you want it to be." He rolled her onto her back and pressed gentle kisses down the length of her throat. "All you have to do is ask." He latched onto her nipple and sucked it into his mouth.

"Is that all?" The words came out breathy. Her head lolled, and she arched her back, urging him to take more.

While his mouth did incredible things to that nipple, his hand cupped the other breast, and he pinched the nipple between his thumb and forefinger, rolling the tip until it formed a tight little bud.

That same hand abandoned her nipple and slid down her torso, skimming across her ribs, coming to rest at the juncture of her thighs.

Maria stilled, her breath caught in her lungs, her core throbbing with the intensity of her desire.

She wanted him to go lower…willed his fingers to curl into her folds and flick that special place only she had been able to tease to a release.

Diego had never touched her there with his fingers, and certainly not with his tongue.

But Venom stopped short. Was that as far as he would go?

Her entire body raged at the injustice.

"Do you want me to go lower?" he asked, his breath warm on her breast.

"Yes," she said, the word rushing out as she released the breath she'd held as his hand rested on her sex. "Please," she said, not at all ashamed of begging for more.

He chuckled and moved lower, his lips searing a path across her skin, igniting her blood and setting her core on fire.

In her mind, she chanted, *Lower. Lower. Lower.*

As his body moved down her length, she parted her legs.

He settled between them, his breath hot on her lady parts, making them tingle in anticipation of what he might do next.

Rough hands, smoothed over her, sliding between her thighs, skimming past her entrance, coming close, but not quite touching her there.

When he stopped petting her, his thumbs brushed across her folds, lifting and separating them to expose the prize lying between them.

Maria's breath hitched, and her hips rose. *There*, she willed. *Touch me there.*

"That's right," he said, his breath warm against her inner thighs. "Tell me what you want."

"Did I say that out loud?" she asked, the words breaking with every erratic breath she couldn't quite pull into her lungs.

He chuckled. "Yes. Be proud. You won't get what you want until you say what you want."

"Oh, sweet Jesus," she cried. "Do I have to tell you everything?" Couldn't he see what he was already doing to her by holding back, teasing her with this insane idea of guiding him to her orgasm?

And why not? Rather than have him fumble around searching for what set her off, she could lead him right to it.

A brilliant concept.

She covered one of his hands with hers and dragged it to the nubbin of flesh containing the key to making her come apart. "There. That's the spot. Touch it, flick it, do whatever it takes to light it up like the fourth of July."

"Now, was that so hard?"

"Yes!" He didn't understand. She'd never asked for what she wanted sexually. Diego would have ignored her request, or worse.

He would have laughed at her.

The man who'd rescued her from recapture and a landslide was rescuing her confidence by allowing her to call the shots and ask for what made her feel good.

Venom parted her folds again and touched that sensitive nubbin with the tip of his finger.

Maria whimpered. "Again."

This time, he flicked her there gently.

Her hips rose. "Don't. Stop." She said between her teeth, her rising desire so strong that breathing became optional. She lay back against the rug, her fingers curling into the shag.

His fingers moved lower to dip into her juices and swirl them around her entrance.

"That's nice, but go back and finish the job," she said, "You can't start something and leave me hanging."

Venom laughed out loud. "Yes, ma'am. On it."

Again he parted her folds. This time, he didn't flick her with his finger. He lowered his head and flicked her clit with his tongue.

An explosion of sensations ripped through the veins just beneath her skin and deep inside.

"Yes," she cried, throwing back her head. "That's the spot. Go! Go! Go!"

He laughed. "I'm not a football player who needs a cheerleader to coach him to the next level."

"I don't care what kind of cheerleader you are or what kind of football player, as long as you hit that spot every time, again and again."

Following her instructions, he licked, flicked and played with that spot until she shot out of orbit and exploded in an orgasm that shook her world.

Riding the crest, she rocked her hips with the pulsing rhythm of her release, slowly floating back to earth. *So, that's what an orgasm feels like.*

Venom laughed. "Surely, that wasn't your first?"

"Did I say that out loud?" What was wrong with her? "I've never felt anything quite that intense in my entire life. As mind-blowing as it was, it leaves me wanting more." She threaded her hands into his hair and tugged gently. "Did you hear me? I want more."

"More what?" he asked, stubbornly forcing her to voice exactly what she wanted him to do to her.

"I want you," she said. "Inside me. Now, damn it."

He tsked his tongue. "Language, pretty mama."

Past patience, she tugged his hair harder.

"Hey, that's my hair." He climbed up her body and kissed her hard. Then he rose on his hands. "Hold that thought, and don't go anywhere."

He flung himself across the shag carpet and snagged a leg of his jeans, dragging them closer. He fished his wallet out of the back pocket, praying his stash of condoms was safely tucked behind his driver's license.

He tore the license out and nearly shouted in triumph. Two condoms. Right where he'd put them. With his treasures in hand, he slid back between Maria's thighs. "Miss me?"

"I did." Maria reached down between them and wrapped her hands around his cock. "And we lost some of our momentum. What will bring it back the quickest?"

She'd turned the tables, now giving him the opportunity to ask for what he wanted.

"I want your mouth on my cock," he said. "If that isn't something you feel comfortable with, don't do it."

Before he finished speaking, she sat up beside him, wrapped her hand around him and bent to flick her tongue across the velvety tip of his member.

It jerked in her hand in reaction to her touch. She did it again. It gave her great satisfaction when it jerked again. Her touch did that. If that was all it took, how would it respond if she wrapped her mouth around him and sucked all of his cock into her mouth?

She lowered her head, flicked the velvety head and ran her tongue around the rim. Then she took him into her mouth and slowly lowered her head until her lips brushed against the base. Reaching out, she fondled his balls, rolling them gently between her fingers, her mouth full of him, her channel weeping in anticipation of that full, thick cock sliding inside her.

She moved up, then back down. Slowly at first, increasing her speed with each stroke.

Venom matched her rhythm, thrusting upward each time. His hands slid over her back and butt, slipping between her legs, a finger dipping into her slick channel.

She moaned around his cock.

He pumped into her mouth faster, his finger sliding into her to the same beat.

Beneath her, his body tensed, and he came to a full stop.

For a moment, he held perfectly still as if gathering what little control he could muster. Then he shoved her off him and came up behind her. He grabbed a condom, tore it open and rolled it over his engorged shaft.

With his hands on her hips, he touched his sheathed cock to her entrance and dipped in and out, wetting the tip. Then he drove into her, burying himself to the hilt.

Maria dropped down to her elbows, rocking back against him.

This was the *more* she'd craved after her own release. "More, Venom," she called out, her voice ragged with desire. "Ride me hard."

His hands gripping her hips, he thrust into her again and again, moving faster and faster until he burst over the edge, his release so powerful his cock throbbed inside her.

When he could finally form a coherent thought, he slid from her channel and pulled her to her knees, leaning her back to his front so that he could cup her full, breasts in his palms.

"Wow," he whispered against her ear. "Not only are you beautiful. You just blew my mind."

She covered his hands on her breasts and moved one down to cup her still pulsing sex. "Is it always this…intense?"

He held her here, dipping a finger in to swirl in her juices, stirring the embers.

"Only if you both want it and are both fully committed to doing it right."

"Mmm." She pressed his finger deeper. "How soon until we can do it again?" Making love with Venom felt so good, so different from what she'd endured at Diego's hand. It felt so good, she couldn't get enough. It was like an addiction she couldn't overcome.

She smiled as he swirled his finger around her

clit, sending sparks to ignite the flame. She'd learned something important about herself.

Being passionate was easy…with the right person.

AFTER MAKING love one more time, Venom insisted they clean up and dress before Sofia woke and asked why they were naked on the floor in the living room.

When Maria and Venom checked on the sleeping child, Sofia opened her eyes and patted the mattress beside her. "Mommy, please stay."

Maria's gaze went to Venom.

He nodded. "Stay."

Sofia was in yet another strange place. Having her mother sleep beside her would help ease her fear of abandonment.

Keyed up, Venom straightened the living room, turned off the fireplace video and wandered into the computer room. The monitor cycled through images from the outside cameras.

Venom watched for a moment, looking at a whole lot of nothing—until something caught his eye. Movement where there shouldn't be movement. He clicked on that camera and watched for the movement again.

There it was again. Dark figures moving around. His pulse quickened, his gut knotting. This wasn't good. The figures out there were people.

"Fuck!"

He reached for the mouse and searched for the

icon on the screen that would allow him to send a text to Jake. He found it, keyed in, "We've got trouble," and hit send.

The figures moving around outside carried flashlights and what looked like large jugs. They were splashing liquid on the weathered boards of the old buildings.

Two of the men pushed over the cast iron pot and yanked at the cables connecting the satellite internet to the computer room.

At the same time, one of the men wielding a jug struck a match and flung it toward the camera. Flames leaped.

The monitors went blank.

Venom ran out of the computer room and into the room where Maria and Sofia slept.

"What's wrong?" Maria whispered in the dark.

"The cartel is here," he said.

Maria was out of the bed and shoving her feet into her boots. "How do you know?"

"I saw them on the monitor."

She switched on the light, found Sofia's shoes and put them on her feet. "How many?"

"A lot." Venom ran to the living room, shoved his feet into his boots, grabbed the shoulder holster, flung it over his shoulders and put his Glock into it. He wrapped the Velcro scabbard around his calf, slid his knife in and covered it with his pants leg. Then he slipped into his leather jacket.

Maria emerged from the bedroom, wearing the

oversized hoodie. She carried Sofia wrapped inside the jacket. "What do we do?"

By that time smoke had penetrated the seals on the automated hatch. The fire could be burning through the gaskets. Before long, it would make its way inside the safe house.

They had to choose between attempting an escape through the escape hatch or moving deeper into the mine. With the smoke increasing, they might not be safe in the mine.

"We have to get out." Venom touched her arm. "I'll go first."

Maria grabbed his hand. "If they see you, they'll kill you."

"We can't stay down here. The smoke will kill us." He caught her cheek in his hand. "We've come this far. They can't stop us now." He kissed her long and hard.

Venom strode into the pantry, grabbed the flashlight hanging on the wall and handed it to Maria. He pushed the shelf aside, exposing the staircase. The smoke wasn't as bad in the stairwell.

If they could get through the trap door without being seen, they could make a run into the darkness. The flames from the burning buildings might blind the cartel thugs, keeping them from seeing into the shadows.

The chance of not being seen was slim, but they had no other choice.

They outnumbered him at least ten to one, maybe more.

Venom climbed the stairs two at a time. When he reached the top, he pulled the Glock from his holster and eased up the trap door. Nothing moved in front of him.

He raised the door enough to slip through onto the old wooden floor. Crouching low, he laid his Glock on the floor, reached for Sofia and lifted her through the trap door.

Maria was halfway through when he turned to help her. She stepped out on her own. When she straightened, she cried, "Look out!"

Venom spun and swung at the man lunging toward him, catching him on the chin. His head snapped back, and he fell against the wall.

Venom didn't give him a chance to regroup and try again. He slammed his fist into his gut. When the guy doubled over, Venom brought up his knee, crashing it into his attacker's face. The guy dropped to the ground and lay still. Venom scooped up his gun and started for the door.

A movement out of the corner of his eye made him glance back in time to see a man dive through the window and roll across the floor.

Before Venom could get a bead on him, the man stopped at Sofia's feet.

Venom couldn't get a clear shot with Sofia in the way.

Maria raised the flashlight in her hand but was too late.

The intruder hooked Sofia's leg with his arm, and she fell into his arms. She fought, wiggling and kicking, until he pressed a knife to her throat. "Move, and I'll kill her."

# CHAPTER 13

"THROW DOWN YOUR GUN," Sofia's captor demanded.

Maria's heart sank to her knees as Venom laid the Glock on the ground.

"Now, kick it toward me."

Once Venom kicked it toward him, the man yelled, "I've got them!"

Venom turned to Sofia. "I'll find you and your mama."

The five-year-old girl, with the maturity of an eighty-year-old man, nodded.

Venom met Maria's gaze in the glow from the nearby fire. "This isn't over."

Her heart lodged in her throat. From the look in his eyes, he meant what had happened between them more so than what was about to go down.

But Venom was unarmed, surrounded by the Valdez cartel known for ruthlessly killing anyone who got in their way. How could it not be over?

By this time, a dozen men had gathered around the old building. Four men entered, grabbed Venom and yanked his arms behind his back. They bound his wrists with a zip tie and dragged him out into the open.

Maria could do nothing to help Venom or her daughter for fear the man with the knife would follow through on his threat and kill Sofia.

When two men grabbed her arms, she didn't struggle, not when Sofia's life depended on her cooperation. Once in the open, the men pulled Maria's wrists behind her back and secured them with a zip tie.

The man with the knife at Sofia's throat carried Sofia out of the building and strode for one of the SUVs heading toward them. He stopped long enough to place Sofia on the ground and pulled another zip tie from his back pocket.

Sofia kicked him in the shin and dashed for freedom. She didn't get far before he caught her again and secured her wrists and ankles. An SUV stopped beside him. He opened the back door, shoved Sofia in and turned to wave for his counterpart to hurry over with Maria.

The fire burning in the first two buildings lit up the night. Men carrying plastic gas jugs poured fuel on the remaining structures.

As she reached the SUV with Sofia inside, Maria glanced over her shoulder, expecting Venom to be herded into their transport vehicles.

Four men held him near one of the buildings they were dousing with gasoline.

Her own abductors pushed her into the SUV and slammed the door.

"Wait," she called out. "You need to bring the other man."

The driver and the man riding shotgun shook their heads, smirking.

The vehicle made a wide turn.

Maria's head swiveled to keep Venom in sight.

The four men dragged him toward the building they'd just doused with gasoline.

He fought the best he could with his hands tied behind his back. Able to break free of their grip, he ducked and rammed his head into one man's gut, knocking him into another. Both men went down. He turned and started toward the others.

He head-butted one, sending him stumbling backward to land on his butt. The other man held a flashlight in his hand.

When Venom bent and charged him, the man raised the flashlight and caught Venom on the chin. The force of the blow sent Venom flying into the wall of the building. He hit headfirst, fell to his knees and swayed.

He staggered to his feet and turned.

The guy with the flashlight swung again.

Venom ducked. The heavy metal light hit him in the temple. He dropped to the ground and lay still.

Two men hooked him beneath his arms and

dragged him into the structure. Moments later, they came out alone.

Another man struck a match and tossed it toward the weathered boards that had once been someone's home. Flames leaped as the gasoline ignited.

Maria cried out. "No! You can't do this. Stop! Please!"

No matter how loud she screamed, they drove away until all she could see was a pale orange glow.

The men didn't chitchat or bullshit. They sat in stony silence.

"How did you find us?" Maria asked, tired but curious and willing to learn from her mistakes.

The man with hazel eyes and a crewcut snorted. "There aren't many secrets in small towns. You just have to listen. One cup of coffee in the local diner, and you know everything that's happened in the last twenty-four hours."

"One cup of coffee?"

He nodded. "A plane dropping off two men is news, especially when they aren't local, and they didn't fly out. Following the plane that landed in Vaughn got us to Colorado Springs and the FBO it calls home. A chat with the receptionist at the desk gave me the unpaid ad for the Brotherhood Protectors based out of the Fool's Gold area. Small towns don't have secrets. My patience paid off when I wandered into a flower shop where the ladies had collected clothes for a woman and her child down on their luck. A female child five years old. I did my part and bought a brand-new pink teddy bear for the child with nothing but the clothes on her back."

Maria's eyes widened. "The pink bear was from you?"

He nodded. "I slipped a tracker through a very small gap in a seam. We knew where she was down to the room where she slept."

Hope took a huge hit. If the cartel had more guys like this working their deliveries, no wonder they were making billions. She hadn't stood a chance of keeping her freedom from the moment she'd climbed out that window.

They drove for eight or ten miles until they came to an open field beside the road. A helicopter stood in the middle with its rotors spinning.

Men dragged Maria out of the SUV. Another carried Sofia. They loaded them on the helicopter and climbed in beside them. The chopper rose from the ground and flew for a while. Maria didn't know how much time had passed. It was as if a giant hand had reached down and grabbed her heart, squeezing so hard she was sure it would cease to beat.

Venom.

A good man who'd put down his gun to keep Sofia from being killed.

They'd left him to die in the fire.

Silent tears slid down her cheeks. She held back the sobs, but the tears kept coming.

"Mommy," Sofia said softly, "it's going to be okay. Mr. Vincent will find us and bring us home."

She hadn't seen what had happened to Venom. She didn't know the man they'd come to trust and love lay unconscious, destined to die in the fire.

Heartsick and past hope, Maria stared into space. She and Sofia would be taken back to Mexico and locked in the Valdez compound. Diego would never let them cross the border again. No one would come to rescue them. They'd have to take on the entire Valdez cartel.

For a very short time, Maria had basked in hope. Hope for a life free of abuse. Free of drug-running criminals who handled most arguments by killing the ones who disagreed with them. For a brief moment, she'd had hope for a normal life for her daughter, surrounded by friends who loved her and protected from people who would hurt her.

And lastly, Maria had dared to hope for herself, for love and real passion.

The helicopter slowed, hovered and descended on a deserted airstrip without a tower.

The three captors pulled Maria and Sofia out of the helicopter and moved them away from the spinning rotors. The aircraft lifted off the ground, leaving them standing in the middle of nowhere, not a building in sight.

"I don't understand," Maria whispered.

The hum of an engine grew louder, coming from somewhere overhead.

Maria scanned the sky for the blinking lights of an airplane and found none. Yet, the aircraft engine noise grew louder. Suddenly, a small jet appeared out of the sky and landed on the narrow landing strip, rolling to a stop several yards away from where Maria and Sofia stood with their jailors.

A man opened the gangway, lowering the steps to the ground.

Her two goons hooked her arms with meaty hands and shoved her toward the plane. Alone, she would have risked death to attempt an escape. With Sofia, she couldn't leave and abandon her to her father's wrath. The odds were against them. Three men against one woman and a little girl didn't give them much of a chance. Her escape from El Paso wouldn't have worked if she'd had three bodyguards watching her every move. Diego wouldn't make that mistake again. Raul had probably paid dearly for allowing her to get away with Sofia.

Once in the air, their zip ties were cut, allowing them to sit comfortably for the duration of the flight.

In the jet, flight time to the border of Mexico didn't take nearly as long as the drive to Colorado. Before long, the plane crossed the border and circled the compound. Lights marked the corners of the six-foot-high concrete fence surrounding the complex, including the warehouses Xavier had built to stage his products.

Though the landing strip was dirt, it was hard-packed, expertly leveled and smoothed. *El Martillo* had had lights installed that could be lit using a special radio frequency.

Suddenly, the lights blinked on, illuminating the landing strip. The pilot lined up with the runway and landed, kicking in the reverse thrusters to slow it quickly and bring it to a complete standstill.

Once the passengers had disembarked, the pilot didn't linger. He had the jet back in the air in a few short minutes.

A large black SUV waited on the hard-packed dirt airfield, its headlights illuminating their path.

As her escorts shoved her forward, the doors of the SUV opened. The driver and front passenger, both dressed in black and armed to the teeth, turned to open the backdoors.

Diego Valdez emerged from one side, and his father, Xavier Valdez, *el Martillo*, the Hammer, stepped out, dressed in a tailored black business suit, wearing high-dollar sunglasses and high-gloss patent leather shoes.

Sofia clung to her mother's hand. "I want to go home," she whispered. "To the Lost Lodge."

Maria's heart clenched at Sofia's shorter version of the Lost Valley Lodge. Her daughter had been happy for the short time she'd been there. The people had been friendly and had gone out of their way to make Maria and Sofia welcome and comfortable.

Unlike the inhabitants of the Valdez compound.

Maria had only seen *El Martillo* on one other occasion, even though she'd frequented the Valdez compound often, overseeing his billion-dollar business. He hadn't gone out of his way to visit his son's prisoner or his granddaughter.

Though the drug lord was barrel-chested, whereas his son was trim, *El Martillo* was at least four inches taller than his son. The father had black hair streaked with silver. Diego looked more like his mother, with light brown hair and green eyes. He handled much of the business on the US side since he blended in so easily.

As El *Martillo* approached, his mouth was set in a thin, pinched line.

Diego's eyes narrowed, his lip curling up in a sneer. "You thought you could just leave and take my daughter." He shook his head. "That's not how it works with the Valdez family."

*El Martillo* lifted his chin and directed the reflection in the lenses of his sunglasses toward Maria. "You've diverted a great deal of resources, causing the delay of several shipments. We cannot allow this to happen again. You will be confined to your quarters until further notice."

"You mean locked in. A prisoner," Maria snorted softly. "Why not let me and Sofia go live our own lives? You won't have to pull resources trying to get us back to assuage hurt pride." She shot a narrow-eyed glare at the man.

"You and Sofia belong to me," Diego bit out.

Maria lifted her chin. "We don't belong to anyone. We're our own people with our own thoughts, feelings, hopes and dreams. And we deserve to be happy and free of fear. A child should never fear being beaten by her parent."

"I hit her once!" Diego's face suffused with a ruddy red.

"And how many times did you hit me?" Maria turned her face toward him, the bruises around her eye vividly telling.

"You don't listen. You contradict everything I say." Diego flung his hand toward her.

Maria flinched but didn't back away.

"You've even turned my daughter against me." He glared at Sofia. "I'm her father."

Her daughter lifted her chin. "You're not my father. Fathers don't hit their little girls. You're Diego."

The younger Valdez's cheeks flushed even redder. "You see? She doesn't like me."

Maria cocked an eyebrow but didn't say a word. Sofia had stated it perfectly.

"Contain them," Xavier ordered in English. He spun and started walking away.

Diego's eyes narrowed. "Try and keep up." Then he turned and hurried after his father, the man in charge. The legendary kingpin running the operation.

His father kept talking, this time in Spanish. "We have deliveries to make. I don't want them in the way. If they cause trouble, I'll deal with them, and they won't expend any more resources then."

Maria's belly clenched, and her hand tightened

around Sofia's. She'd understood every word. *El Martillo* didn't threaten, he acted. He'd earned his reputation by eliminating the competition and anyone who stood in the way of what he wanted.

Since his son hadn't handled the situation well with Maria and Sofia, his father would take charge the next time. After that, there would be no next time.

The SUV Diego and his father had arrived in left with their original passengers, none more.

Another SUV arrived, and Maria and Sofia were loaded into it and transported to the compound. Maria was escorted to a single bedchamber with an adjoining bathroom. When she entered, a guard held Sofia back and shut the door.

"Wait! Let me have my daughter!" Maria pounded her fists against the door, but they didn't listen. They had their orders, no doubt.

She listened to their footsteps on the Saltillo tile floors. They stopped at the next door.

Keys jingled and scraped inside a lock. Door hinges creaked when it opened and when it closed.

When the guards walked away, their footsteps fading, Maria called out, "Sofia, are you okay?"

"I want to go home," she said. "I don't like this place."

"We're going to be all right, *mija*." Maria didn't know how things would ever be all right, but she didn't want Sofia to give up hope.

"I know," Sofia said with the confidence of a five-year-old. "Mr. Vincent said he'd find us. When he does, he'll take us home."

Ready tears welled in her eyes. One night. They'd only had one night together before…

Her throat swelled with repressed sobs.

"Mommy, don't cry," Sofia said.

How did she know? Maria had tried not to sob out loud. Had she sniffled? The child had to be psychic.

"We're going to get out of here," Sofia said softly but loud enough Maria could hear her through the walls and doors. "Mr. Vincent is going to teach me how to swim and fish. I've gone all my life without learning how to swim."

"That's a long time," Maria agreed, her lips twitching.

"Do you think Mr. Vincent can ride a bike?"

She didn't have the heart to tell Sofia that Mr. Vincent was most likely…dead. She could hardly believe it herself. "Are you going to ask him to teach you how to do that, too?"

"Yes. I like him," she responded. "Do you think, if I asked him, that he would be my daddy?"

"Mr. Vincent is a busy man. He might not have time to teach you all of that. It takes lots of practice to do some of these things." Maria had to get Sofia's mind off Venom. The more they talked about him, the more her heart ached.

Everything about their night together was still with her, fresh. Down to the whisker burn on the insides of her thighs. Her breath hitched. She couldn't stand around crying. She needed something else to focus on.

"I'm going to get out of here," Sofia announced. "When I do, I'm going to get you out, too."

Maria's heart swelled. Sofia had a big heart, and she hated it when others were lonely, sad or hurt.

"You should try to rest. You were very sick yesterday, and we don't have your medicine to keep you from getting sick again."

"I'm not sleepy," she said and yawned.

Maria laughed. "Lay down and sleep. Rest helps you think better."

"If I rest, I might think of a way to get out of here."

"That's right, *mija*. Sleep," Maria said. "We can worry about escaping tomorrow."

For a few minutes, Sofia was silent. "Mommy, I'm going back to Lost Lodge. But first, I'm going to take a nap. When I wake up, I'll think better and find a way out of here."

"Okay, *chica*. I'm here if you need to talk."

Maria dozed, making use of what was left of the night to rest. As discouraged as she was by her failed attempt at gaining her and Sofia's freedom, that little taste of a better life had left her wanting more. She couldn't imagine it now without Venom there.

# CHAPTER 14

As soon as the men who'd dragged Venom into the old building let go of their hold on him, he hit the hard weathered-wood floor, which jolted him back to consciousness. He played dead until the men walked out. As long as they thought he was dead, he had a chance.

Then they lit up his world, making it even more imperative that he get out ASAP. His wrists bound behind him slowed him down, but they hadn't tied his ankles. He just had to get to his feet and find another way out without going through the front door where the dozen or so cartel thugs stood around admiring their pyrotechnics.

The fire spread fast, burning through the gallons of fuel they'd poured on the weathered wood. As old as it was, the wood was kindling in the flames. It wouldn't be long before everything was consumed.

He just had to make sure he wasn't included in

that consumption and do his best to avoid being shot. These guys didn't appear to be the patient types. If they had to kill you more than once, they'd probably go for the more direct method that gave immediate, definitive results, like a bullet to the head.

Nope. He couldn't let that happen. The cartel had his girls, and he'd promised to find them. A little girl was counting on him. And he had a lot of unfinished business with her mother.

Venom managed to get to his feet and run to the back of the building. There were no windows to jump out of and no door. The fire burned hotter behind him but had yet to spread to the back.

If he could break through a wall…

He backed up and ran at the back wall, turning at the last minute and hitting it with his shoulder.

He bounced off the hundred-year-old planks and landed flat on his ass. If the boards had lasted through all those years of harsh elements and still stood, ramming them like a football linebacker would have little effect. He had to act fast or die. Flames had burned through the gasoline quickly. Hopefully, it might take longer to consume the petrified planks.

He peered through the front room. Both sides had a window and the front had two windows and the door.

Cartel arsonists danced in the firelight, slinging the last drops of gas into the flames. So, the front was out. "Side window it is," he murmured to himself.

Both side windows were like rings of fire, the hole in the center providing no fuel for the hungry flames. If he dove through with his hands secured behind his back, he might land on his head and die of a broken neck. If he tried to step through one, his pants could catch fire. He might burn some important parts, but he couldn't risk breaking his neck. Smoke burned his eyes and lungs the longer he waited.

Venom ran through the burning room, squinting to spare his eyes. As he reached a window, he shoved a leg through, ended up sitting on the burning windowsill, ducked his head and flung himself out onto the ground. He rolled into a sitting position and scooted across the dirt, extinguishing anything that might still be burning.

Shouts rose from the men fueling the fires. Engines revved, and headlights spun in circles as the attackers vacated the scene of their crimes.

Soon, the only lights shining were the fires burning away at the buildings that formed the ghost town. Venom looked around for something sharp he could use to break the zip tie holding his wrists behind him. He spotted the cast iron pot and hurried over. Half-sitting on the edge, he rubbed the plastic binding over the pot's rim. Finally, the tie broke, and he was free.

Free, with neither a cell phone, radio or vehicle. The longer he took getting started, the further away Maria and Sofia would go.

The Valdez cartel would return them to Diego at

their compound in Mexico. The sooner Venom got there, the sooner he could fulfill his promise to find them. He'd worry about how to rescue them once he got there. One step at a time.

He took the first step, heading down the road to the safe house. He'd gone halfway down when headlights shone through the trees, bouncing up the rutted path.

Not wanting to wrestle with another dozen cartel thugs, he stepped into the brush and waited for the vehicle to go by to determine whether they were friend or foe. He had sent a message to Jake before all hell broke loose. Had he had enough time to get back out here?

The vehicle bounced erratically, moving faster than the rutted road allowed.

Venom watched as it drove past. He could just make out the driver.

JoJo.

The SUV had almost left him behind when he burst out of the brush and pounded on the back window.

The brake light came on, and the vehicle slammed to a halt.

All four doors burst open. Every person who leaped out held a gun pointed at him.

Venom's hands shot into the air. "It's me, Venom! Don't shoot!"

"Holy shit, Ven." JoJo lowered her handgun and

scrubbed a hand down her face. "I nearly had a coronary."

Max, Weaver and Tayo shook their heads as one.

"We almost popped you," Max said. "Never do that again."

"They're all gone up top. I had to be sure they hadn't come back," Venom said. "Get in and turn this vehicle around."

They all piled in.

JoJo spun the big SUV around, taking out several small saplings in the process.

"I don't know if the fire spread to the rooms below, but the smoke had. We had to make a run for it. Unfortunately, there were more than a dozen of them and only one of me. I came out, firing. One of them dove through a window and took Sofia hostage, threatening to kill her if I didn't give up my gun." He clenched his teeth. "They took them. They smoked us out and snatched the girls."

"Take comfort in the fact they took them alive," Max said. "If they'd wanted to kill them, they would have done it then."

"You think they're taking them back to Mexico?" JoJo glanced into the rearview mirror.

"That would be my guess." Venom pounded his fist into his palm. "We have to get to Mexico. Jake, what aircraft—" He looked around. "Where's Jake?"

"He's been holed up in the war room since he dropped you at the safe house," Max said. "He chased all of us out. Said he'd fill us in when he could. Apparently, something big is about to go down, and I think we're going to be involved. He put the entire team on standby. They're gathered at the lodge, waiting for orders."

When JoJo reached the highway, she slammed the accelerator to the floor and broke every speed limit getting to and through Fool's Gold. As she slowed to take the turn to Lost Valley Ranch, Max held up his hand. "Hold up." He stared at his cell phone, reading a text that had just come through. He looked up and pointed at the road straight ahead. "Colorado Springs Airport."

JoJo frowned, straightened the wheel and hit the gas again.

"Why the airport?" Weaver asked.

"Probably has something to do with what Hank has going on." Max stared down at the message again. "It would be nice to know what's going on." His phone pinged with an incoming text. He frowned as he read. "It's from Cole. He says they left for the airport fifteen minutes ago and will see us there."

Venom shook his head. "I'm going to Mexico. If Hank's mission happens to get us to Valdez's compound, I'm on board. Otherwise, I'll find my own way. I promised Maria and Sofia I'd find them. I'm not breaking my damned promise."

The drive to the airport seemed to take forever. He had no idea where Maria and Sofia were by now. Did the cartel have their own plane, or would they transport them by road?

If he could have paced, he would have. Sitting in a vehicle twiddling his thumbs wasn't the action he needed.

Where were they?

As they entered Colorado Springs, Max received a text telling them which part of the airport to go to.

When they arrived, they entered a private hangar where the rest of the Colorado team had gathered with Jake standing at the center.

When Jake had their attention, he spoke clearly. "I'm taking you all into the conference center where you'll be asked to sign an NDA, non-disclosure agreement, for the mission we're about to undertake." When everyone started talking at once, Jake held up his hand. "You'll get all the information in the preflight briefing. If anyone wants out, now is the time to say so."

Venom held up his hand. "They have Maria and Sofia. I'll go anywhere they've taken them, otherwise, I'm out, and I'll find my own way."

Jake nodded. "Anyone else?"

Silence.

Staring hard at Venom, he said, "Everyone, follow me."

Venom took that to mean whatever this op was, it involved Maria and Sofia, so he prepared to follow Hank.

Jake started for the door at the far end of the hanger, stopped and fixed the shortest person in the group with a frown. "JoJo? Are you coming as a Brotherhood Protector?"

She nodded. "I'll come as the goddamn Easter Bunny if it gets me anywhere close to Maria and her kid."

"Ever jump?" he asked.

She frowned. "No, but I learn quickly."

Jake shook his head. "This won't be the place to learn. Sorry. You're out."

JoJo glared at him and stepped back, allowing the others to file into the large conference room.

Venom was surprised to see fifteen or more people already there, including Hank and Swede, whom he knew only from the video calls they did often to help out or catch up. Hank crossed the room to where Venom stood and held out his hand. "I'm glad you're okay. I hear you had a little trouble with the safe house."

Venom nodded. "They smoked us out, grabbed the kid and used her as a hostage."

"Well, we hope to get them back in Joint Operation Whiplash." Hank glanced around the room of faces and lifted his chin. "We're working closely with the DEA, Customs and Border Patrol and Homeland Security to locate, confiscate and detain a huge shipment of drugs scheduled to ship tonight via tractor-trailer rigs. They'll cross the border in different locations and head north with stops along the way. The goal is to shut down the Valdez drug pipeline and bring in all the people supporting it."

"How do we fit into this picture?" Max asked.

"While the DEA is tagging the logistics connections, we're going in to hit the command and support center of their operations. Our goal is to capture or eliminate their top-tier decision-makers."

"Diego and Xavier Valdez," Venom filled in, grinding his teeth together at the mention of the bastard who'd stolen Maria and Sofia when all they wanted was to live normal lives. "I'm in," Venom said.

Hank dipped his head. "Satellite images indicate the compound is fortified, heavily guarded and armed, whichever way you look at it. I've brought every weapon we'll need and a few more, just in case. Each man will wear body armor and a helmet with a headset."

He paused and looked around at his group from Montana and Jake's from Colorado. "Since our government highly discourages launching combat missions into countries with whom we share a border, we'll be super careful not to be real obvious about it. We're dropping equipment and jumping in."

"We have enough chutes?" Tayo said.

Hank nodded. "We'll be dropped from the plane on the US side of the airspace and float into Mexico with our equipment, which includes all-terrain vehicles, side-by-sides and dirt bikes. You might share a vehicle with other team members. It doesn't matter. What matters is that we all get to the compound by midnight, at which time we'll breach the walls, go in and clean up. Between the transportation movement and breaching the compound, our goal is to capture, eliminate and neutralize the Valdez cartel."

"I feel like I'm back in the Army," Cole said. "Let's do this!"

Over the next few hours, the team distributed weapons, ammo, body armor, radios and more.

Tayo and several others inspected the parachutes that had been professionally packed and inspected.

Their transportation to the drop zone was the C-130 parked outside the hangar, complete with a pilot, co-pilot and loadmaster who helped them move the equipment on board and double-checked the parachutes that would deliver them to the ground.

When it was time to go, they were suited, safety briefed and familiarized with the items they would take into battle.

The extraction plan was to drive back across the border. A select group of Customs and Border Patrol officers would ensure they passed through without issue. They were to initiate contact at midnight and be back across the border before sunrise.

The mission was so top secret they were required to leave all forms of identification behind. If interrogated, they were to deny any connection to the US government.

Thirty men loaded into the C-130 aircraft and strapped into their chutes, armed to the teeth and pumped.

The flight from Colorado Springs to the drop

zone would have them jumping at dusk and landing in the dark.

Venom was ready. He was assigned a dirt bike to get him to the compound. When they found Maria and Sofia, he'd bring them out in a side-by-side all-terrain utility vehicle.

The weather was clear, with no significant wind to blow them off course.

The flight passed quicker than Venom would have thought. He spent the time going over satellite images of the compound they'd been shown. Their informant on the inside had diagrammed the different sections, indicating the living quarters of the cartel leadership, barracks, storerooms, holding cells, fuel tanks and the warehouse where product was stored with a loose attempt to disguise it as Mexican pottery.

Venom, Jake, Tayo, Weaver, Max and Sawyer were tasked with extracting Maria and Sofia. Venom would take point.

As they neared the drop zone, the ramp lowered. One by one, they pushed the all-terrain vehicles out into the night sky.

The men deployed, filling the sky with chutes.

Suddenly, Venom was out of the plane, his parachute deployed and drifting through a quiet sky into Mexico.

When he touched down, he rolled up his chute and stepped out of the harness. He found one of the dirt bikes lying on its side. After untangling it from its parachute and protective packaging, he straddled the seat and started the engine.

One by one, the team reported in as they located their equipment and tested that it was still operational after the drop. Slowly, the chaos leveled out, and the team set out cross-country on schedule to arrive at the compound at midnight.

Venom and the extraction team led the pack. They planned a stealth infiltration ahead of the rest of the team.

Then they were there, overlooking the compound from a low ridge half a mile away.

If all went as planned, the operation would kick off fifteen minutes before midnight for the extraction team and midnight for everyone else, supposedly including the DEA, Border Patrol and Homeland Security components poised to intercept a huge shipment of drugs headed north under the guise of being Mexican pottery and medical supplies.

Hank and a team of his guys from Montana would focus on capturing the leaders, including Diego and Xavier Valdez.

Venom hoped the Valdez's drew first fire. Maria and Sofia would never be free until Diego and his father were dead.

If given the opportunity, Venom would make that happen.

However, his first priority was to find his girls.

# CHAPTER 15

"Mommy, I slept, and it did help me be smarter."

"How so, *mija?*" Maria asked, wishing their voices weren't so muffled by the walls between them. Sofia was awake well past her bedtime. It had to be getting close to midnight.

"There's a window that looks into a garden. I pushed my bed up to it. I'm little; I might fit through the bars."

Maria frowned. "Wait…what bars?"

"On the window. I'm going to climb through."

"Oh, baby, please be careful."

"I will."

Silence followed.

"Sofia?"

No response.

Maria paced the length of her room, her heart in her throat. What would they do to the little girl if they caught her roaming the halls?

Trapped in her cell of a room, she could do nothing to help.

More minutes passed. "Sofia? *Mija*? Please tell me you're okay."

A sound in the hallway made Maria's heart stop.

She had no idea what would happen if their guards found Sofia missing. Xavier Valdez had promised to put an end to the trouble they'd caused.

Something bumped against her door, and the sound of the latch that locked the door in place sliding open had Maria bracing herself to fight for her life and her daughter's.

Another bump sounded against the door, and suddenly, it opened. Sofia stood with her hand on the doorknob. She waved for Maria to follow her. "Come on. We're going home."

Bless her heart. She had no idea how hard it would be to get out of the compound. The number of guards armed with automatic weapons terrified her. Would they shoot a child?

With no idea which way to go, Maria followed her daughter, pausing at corners to see if the coast was clear.

At first, the hallways were quiet, with no one moving about.

Then footsteps echoed off the walls as someone ran toward them from another corridor.

Maria found a door that wasn't locked and pushed Sofia and herself through, closing it almost all the way before the runner passed.

Another person ran from the same direction, heading where the other runner had gone.

Maria looked around. They were in a supply closet. The back wall had another door. She opened it to find what appeared to be living quarters with a sofa, reading lamp and a Persian rug on the floor. Sofia stepped into the room before Maria could stop her. She crossed to a door on the other side and pushed it open.

Maria hurried after her.

The room was an office with a mahogany desk in the center.

Her heart fluttered. If she had to guess, they'd walked right into *El Martillo's* private office and living quarters.

"Sofia, we have to get out of here. This is Mr. Valdez's office. Diego's father."

"It's okay. He's not in here." She crossed to another door.

Maria caught her before she opened that one, too. "Sofia, we have to get out of here right now."

Voices carried from the other side of the door Sofia had her hand on, and they were headed toward them. Maria snatched up her daughter and ducked behind the massive desk, squeezing beneath the knee space. She pulled the office chair toward her and Sofia.

The door they'd been standing in front of a moment before slammed open. Two men entered, arguing.

Maria peered through a slim gap in the panel and smothered a gasp.

Diego and his father stood in the office, their faces angry, each holding a gun pointed at the other.

They were arguing in Spanish, speaking so fast Maria could barely keep up. They were angry about the shipment. Something was wrong. The trucks had been intercepted. Diego blamed his father, claiming he was living in the past. His father blamed Diego for wasting time on an American woman, and for what? His pride? He was a disappointment to the Valdez name.

Diego grabbed for his father's gun.

Maria shielded Sophia with her body as two shots were fired, and then silence followed.

Maria sat up and peered through the gap but couldn't see anything. The room appeared empty, but she couldn't see the floor through the gap.

After a long silence, she pushed the chair slowly away from them, scooted out from under the desk and peeked around the side.

Her breath caught.

Lying on the floor as still as death lay Xavier Valdez. But where was Diego?

Xavier's body lay in front of the supply door, blocking it as an exit.

The only way out was through the door the two men had entered.

Maria took Sofia's hand and inched around the body on the floor to get to the open door.

As she passed the dead man's right hand, she noticed his gun beneath it.

Maria had fired rifles and handguns when she'd been on active duty. So she understood how they worked and the basics of marksmanship. But it was a dead man's gun.

She started to step past it but stopped, leaned down and slid it out from under his hand. She tucked it into the waistband of her jeans and pulled her gray sweater over it.

After a quick look around the doorframe, Maria led Sofia through what appeared to be a small conference room. The door stood open to a hallway beyond the room.

Footsteps hurried toward the doorway.

Maria and Sofia dropped to the floor and crawled beneath the small conference table. Legs passed in front of them.

Sofia whispered, "Diego."

He entered his father's office and stepped over the body on the floor. When he came back out, he carried a thick wad of cash. A 100-dollar bill slipped out and fluttered to the floor.

Maria froze.

For a moment, she thought he might not notice. Then he bent and picked up the bill. When he started to rise, he looked straight into Maria's eyes.

"What the hell?" He reached beneath the table, grabbed her arm and dragged her out.

Maria prayed Sofia remained hidden.

"How did you get out? That door was locked from the outside." Still holding her arm, he stepped out into the hall. "Did someone let you out?"

Maria shook her head. "No. The lock was secure. I shook it until it opened on its own."

"Bullshit," he said. "My father let you out, didn't he?"

She shook her head. "No." Her gaze shot to the door through which his father's body was clearly visible. "Why did you shoot him?"

"He was an arrogant bastard. He thought his way was the only way. He didn't understand why I had to get you and the kid back. The people who work for us would never respect me if I let you leave. It's not just about pride. You can't lead if you can't command respect." He glared down at her, his grip on her arm tightening painfully.

"And you never understood respect. You think you're better than me. Just like my father." He jerked her arm. "Well, you're not better than me. You're a cold, passionless bitch. I've had better sex with whores."

Maria strained against his hold. "Let go of my arm."

"Or what?" He jerked her again. "Or nothing. You can do nothing. I'm in control, not you." He pulled her close against him and groped her breast.

"The problem isn't me," Maria said. "I'm a very passionate woman. Just not with you."

Diego slapped the side of her head so hard her ears rang.

A flash of movement darted from beneath the conference table, and Sofia threw herself at Diego. "Don't hit my Mommy. You're not my father; Mr. Vincent is. You're just a mean man."

Diego let go of Maria and caught Sofia by the hair. "I'll show you who's your father." He pulled her into his arms and wrapped his arm around her neck. "How's that feel."

Sofia clawed at the arm, fighting to breathe.

Maria rushed toward Diego. "Let her go."

"No. She belongs to me. I can do anything I want with her."

"She can't breathe!" Maria cried. "Let her go! Or I'll…I'll…"

"You'll what?" He sneered. "You're pathetic."

Maria pulled the gun from her waistband and aimed it at Diego's head. "Let her go, or I'll shoot you."

Diego laughed. "You won't shoot me. What if you miss and hit your precious brat?" He held out his other hand. "Give me the gun."

"I know how to shoot. I was an expert shot in the Army. I will shoot you. Let. Her. Go."

Sofia's face had gone from a healthy tan to blue.

Maria raised the gun and aimed it at Diego's sneering face. She rested her finger on the trigger and took a steadying breath…

A shot rang out.

Maria's finger hadn't applied any pressure. Had the weapon misfired?

She stared in horror at her daughter as she fell from Diego's grasp, blood coating her hair.

Diego's eyes rounded, and he raised his hand to his throat, where blood gushed with each beat of his heart. He reached for her and then crumpled to the floor.

A sound made her look to the door.

Venom slowly lowered his pistol.

"Oh, God... Sofia!" Maria lunged toward her daughter.

Before she could reach her, the little girl launched herself at Venom.

He caught her up in one arm and hugged her close, tears in his eyes.

"You found us," Sofia said, burying her face in his neck while her arms wrapped tightly around his neck.

"I found you," he said, his voice cracking.

Maria staggered toward him.

He pulled her against him and pressed a kiss to her temple.

Two men stepped up behind him. Maria recognized Jake.

The other man nodded. "I'm Hank. I'm with these guys." He stepped into the office, glanced down at Diego's still body and moved into the office where Xavier Valdez lay dead. "Not only did you find our girls, you accomplished the other part of our mission." He patted Venom's back. "Let's get out of here."

Venom looked from Sofia to Maria. "Are you ready to go home?"

Sofia gave a resounding, "Yes!"

Maria nodded.

Venom grinned. "Then get ready for a wild ride."

# EPILOGUE

"THIS ONE WAS JUST LISTED TODAY." Venom pushed the door open and stood back for Maria and Sofia to enter the house he'd found at the end of a cul-de-sac in Fool's Gold.

Maria's eyes widened. "It's beautiful."

Venom grinned. "I thought you'd like it. It has all the windows you could possibly want, plus a big backyard with a fence."

Sofia clapped her hands. "Does that mean we can have a puppy?"

Venom shrugged. "If your mama is okay with it."

Sofia launched herself at him, wrapping her arm around his leg. "I love you, Mr. Vincent."

He picked her up and kissed her cheek. "I love you, too, Sofia."

She grinned and pressed a kiss to his cheek. "Since we're getting a house together, does that mean you're going to marry my mommy?"

Venom laughed. "Trust the five-year-old to steal my thunder." He held out his hand.

Maria slipped hers into it.

"I don't have a ring yet, and I planned on a candlelit dinner with wine and music, and I'll still do all that, but the cat's out of the bag, and people want to know." He lifted her hand to his lips. "Maria Elena, we've only known each other for two and a half months, but I knew almost as soon as we met that you were the one for me. You'd make me the happiest man in the world if you'd be my wife."

She laughed up at him and kissed his lips. "I would love to be your wife." She raised an eyebrow. "But I want a rain check on the dinner and ring."

"Done."

Sofia clapped her hands. "If you marry my Mommy, does that mean you'll be my daddy?" She stared into his eyes. "Please?"

"Is that okay with your mommy?"

Maria nodded. "Absolutely!"

"Then Sofia, would you be my daughter, to have and to hold forever and ever?"

"Yes!" Sofia wrapped her arms around his neck and hugged him so tight.

Venom's heart swelled. "Never did I ever dream life could be so good."

"Is that right?" Maria leaned into him, her body warm against his.

"With you two women in my life, it can't get better," he said.

"No?" Maria cocked an eyebrow. "Would another baby make it worse?"

He laughed. "Okay. Point made. A brother or sister for Sofia would make life even better."

Maria ran a finger along his jaw. "Then we'd better get started on that plan."

He waggled his eyebrows. "Have I shown you the master bedroom?"

# BREAKING SILENCE

## DELTA FORCE STRONG

*New York Times* & *USA Today*
Bestselling Author

**ELLE JAMES**

# BREAKING Silence

DELTA FORCE STRONG

New York Times & USA Today Bestselling Author

# ELLE JAMES

# CHAPTER 1

HAD he known they would be deployed so soon after their last short mission to El Salvador, Rucker Sloan wouldn't have bought that dirt bike from his friend Duff. Now, it would sit there for months before he actually got to take it out to the track.

The team had been given forty-eight hours to pack their shit, take care of business and get onto the C130 that would transport them to Afghanistan.

Now, boots on the ground, duffel bags stowed in their assigned quarters behind the wire, they were ready to take on any mission the powers that be saw fit to assign.

What he wanted most that morning, after being awake for the past thirty-six hours, was a cup of strong, black coffee.

The rest of his team had hit the sack as soon as they got in. Rucker had already met with their commanding officer, gotten a brief introduction to the regional issues and had been told to get some rest. They'd be operational within the next forty-eight hours.

Too wound up to sleep, Rucker followed a stream of people he hoped were heading for the chow hall. He should be able to get coffee there.

On the way, he passed a sand volleyball court where two teams played against each other. One of the teams had four players, the other only three. The four-person squad slammed a ball to the ground on the other side of the net. The only female player ran after it as it rolled toward Rucker.

He stopped the ball with his foot and picked it up.

The woman was tall, slender, blond-haired and blue-eyed. She wore an Army PT uniform of shorts and an Army T-shirt with her hair secured back from her face in a ponytail seated on the crown of her head.

Without makeup, and sporting a sheen of perspiration, she was sexy as hell, and the men on both teams knew it.

They groaned when Rucker handed her the ball. He'd robbed them of watching the female soldier bending over to retrieve the runaway.

She took the ball and frowned. "Do you play?"

"I have," he answered.

"We could use a fourth." She lifted her chin in challenge.

Tired from being awake for the past thirty-six hours, Rucker opened his mouth to say *hell no*. But he made the mistake of looking into her sky-blue eyes and instead said, "I'm in."

What the hell was he thinking?

Well, hadn't he been wound up from too many hours sitting in transit? What he needed was a little physical activity to relax his mind and muscles. At least, that's what he told himself in the split-second it took to step into the sandbox and serve up a heaping helping of whoop-ass.

He served six times before the team playing opposite finally returned one. In between each serve, his side gave him high-fives, all members except one— the blonde with the blue eyes he stood behind, admiring the length of her legs beneath her black Army PT shorts.

Twenty minutes later, Rucker's team won the match. The teams broke up and scattered to get showers or breakfast in the chow hall.

"Can I buy you a cup of coffee?" the pretty blonde asked.

"Only if you tell me your name." He twisted his lips into a wry grin. "I'd like to know who delivered those wicked spikes."

She held out her hand. "Nora Michaels," she said.

He gripped her hand in his, pleased to feel firm pressure. Women might be the weaker sex, but he didn't like a dead fish handshake from males or females. Firm and confident was what he preferred. Like her ass in those shorts.

She cocked an eyebrow. "And you are?"

He'd been so intent thinking about her legs and ass, he'd forgotten to introduce himself. "Rucker Sloan. Just got in less than an hour ago."

"Then you could probably use a tour guide to the nearest coffee."

He nodded. "Running on fumes here. Good coffee will help."

"I don't know about good, but it's coffee and it's fresh." She released his hand and fell in step beside him, heading in the direction of some of the others from their volleyball game.

"As long as it's strong and black, I'll be happy."

She laughed. "And awake for the next twenty-four hours."

"Spoken from experience?" he asked, casting a glance in her direction.

She nodded. "I work nights in the medical facility. It can be really boring and hard to stay awake when we don't have any patients to look after." She held up her hands. "Not that I want any of our boys injured and in need of our care."

"But it does get boring," he guessed.

"It makes for a long deployment." She held out her hand. "Nice to meet you, Rucker. Is Rucker a call sign or your real name?"

He grinned. "Real name. That was the only thing my father gave me before he cut out and left my mother and me to make it on our own."

"Your mother raised you, and you still joined the

Army?" She raised an eyebrow. "Most mothers don't want their boys to go off to war."

"It was that or join a gang and end up dead in a gutter," he said. "She couldn't afford to send me to college. I was headed down the gang path when she gave me the ultimatum. Join and get the GI-Bill, or she would cut me off and I'd be out in the streets. To her, it was the only way to get me out of L.A. and to have the potential to go to college someday."

She smiled "And you stayed in the military."

He nodded. "I found a brotherhood that was better than any gang membership in LA. For now, I take college classes online. It was my mother's dream for me to graduate college. She never went, and she wanted so much more for me than the streets of L.A.. When my gig is up with the Army, if I haven't finished my degree, I'll go to college fulltime."

"And major in what?" Nora asked.

"Business management. I'm going to own my own security service. I want to put my combat skills to use helping people who need dedicated and specialized protection."

Nora nodded. "Sounds like a good plan."

"I know the protection side of things. I need to learn the business side and business law. Life will be different on the civilian side."

"True."

"How about you? What made you sign up?" he asked.

She shrugged. "I wanted to put my nursing degree

to good use and help our men and women in uniform. This is my first assignment after training."

"Drinking from the firehose?" Rucker stopped in front of the door to the mess hall.

She nodded. "Yes. But it's the best baptism under fire medical personnel can get. I'll be a better nurse for it when I return to the States."

"How much longer do you have to go?" he asked, hoping that she'd say she'd be there as long as he was. In his case, he never knew how long their deployments would last. One week, one month, six months…

She gave him a lopsided smile. "I ship out in a week."

"That's too bad." He opened the door for her. "I just got here. That doesn't give us much time to get to know each other."

"That's just as well." Nora stepped through the door. "I don't want to be accused of fraternizing. I'm too close to going back to spoil my record."

Rucker chuckled. "Playing volleyball and sharing a table while drinking coffee won't get you written up. I like the way you play. I'm curious to know where you learned to spike like that."

"I guess that's reasonable. Coffee first." She led him into the chow hall.

The smells of food and coffee made Rucker's mouth water.

He grabbed a tray and loaded his plate with eggs, toast and pancakes drenched in syrup. Last, he stopped at the coffee urn and filled his cup with freshly brewed black coffee.

When he looked around, he found Nora seated at one of the tables, holding a mug in her hands, a small plate with cottage cheese and peaches on it.

He strode over to her. "Mind if I join you?"

"As long as you don't hit on me," she said with cocked eyebrows.

"You say that as if you've been hit on before."

She nodded and sipped her steaming brew. "I lost count how many times in the first week I was here."

"Shows they have good taste in women and, unfortunately, limited manners."

"And you're better?" she asked, a smile twitching the corners of her lips.

"I'm not hitting on you. You can tell me to leave, and I'll be out of this chair so fast, you won't have time to enunciate the V."

She stared straight into his eyes, canted her head to one side and said, "Leave."

In the middle of cutting into one of his pancakes, Rucker dropped his knife and fork on the tray, shot out of his chair and left with his tray, sloshing coffee as he moved. He hoped she was just testing him. If she wasn't...oh, well. He was used to eating meals alone. If she was, she'd have to come to him.

He took a seat at the next table, his back to her, and resumed cutting into his pancake.

Nora didn't utter a word behind him.

Oh, well. He popped a bite of syrupy sweet

pancake in his mouth and chewed thoughtfully. She was only there for another week. Man, she had a nice ass…and those legs… He sighed and bent over his plate to stab his fork into a sausage link.

"This chair taken?" a soft, female voice sounded in front of him.

He looked up to see the pretty blond nurse standing there with her tray in her hands, a crooked smile on her face.

He lifted his chin in silent acknowledgement.

She laid her tray on the table and settled onto the chair. "I didn't think you'd do it."

"Fair enough. You don't know me," he said.

"I know that you joined the Army to get out of street life. That your mother raised you after your father skipped out, that you're working toward a business degree and that your name is Rucker." She sipped her coffee.

He nodded, secretly pleased she'd remembered all that. Maybe there was hope for getting to know the pretty nurse before she redeployed to the States. And who knew? They might run into each other on the other side of the pond.

Still, he couldn't show too much interest, or he'd be no better than the other guys who'd hit on her. "Since you're redeploying back to the States in a week, and I'm due to go out on a mission, probably within the next twenty-four to forty-eight hours, I don't know if it's worth our time to get to know each other any more than we already have."

She nodded. "I guess that's why I want to sit with you. You're not a danger to my perfect record of no fraternizing. I don't have to worry that you'll fall in love with me in such a short amount of time." She winked.

He chuckled. "As I'm sure half of this base has fallen in love with you since you've been here."

She shrugged. "I don't know if it's love, but it's damned annoying."

"How so?"

She rolled her eyes toward the ceiling. "I get flowers left on my door every day."

"And that's annoying? I'm sure it's not easy coming up with flowers out here in the desert." He set down his fork and took up his coffee mug. "I think it's sweet." He held back a smile. Well, almost.

"They're hand-drawn on notepad paper and left on the door of my quarters and on the door to the shower tent." She shook her head. "It's kind of creepy and stalkerish."

Rucker nodded. "I see your point. The guys should at least have tried their hands at origami flowers, since the real things are scarce around here."

Nora smiled. "I'm not worried about the pictures, but the line for sick call is ridiculous."

"How so?"

"So many of the guys come up with the lamest excuses to come in and hit on me. I asked to work the nightshift to avoid sick call altogether."

"You have a fan group." He smiled. "Has the adoration gone to your head?"

She snorted softly. "No."

"You didn't get this kind of reaction back in the States?"

"I haven't been on active duty for long. I only decided to join the Army after my mother passed away. I was her fulltime nurse for a couple years as she went through stage four breast cancer. We thought she might make it." Her shoulders sagged. "But she didn't."

"I'm sorry to hear that. My mother meant a lot to me, as well. I sent money home every month after I enlisted and kept sending it up until the day she died suddenly of an aneurysm."

"I'm so sorry about your mother's passing," Nora said, shaking her head. "Wow. As an enlisted man, how did you make enough to send some home?"

"I ate in the chow hall and lived on post. I didn't party or spend money on civilian clothes or booze. Mom needed it. I gave it to her."

"You were a good son to her," Nora said.

His chest tightened. "She died of an aneurysm a couple of weeks before she was due to move to Texas where I'd purchased a house for her."

"Wow. And, let me guess, you blame yourself for not getting her to Texas sooner...?" Her gaze captured his.

Her words hit home, and he winced. "Yeah. I should've done it sooner."

"Can't bring people back with regrets." Nora stared into her coffee cup. "I learned that. The only thing I could do was move forward and get on with living. I wanted to get away from Milwaukee and the home I'd shared with my mother. Not knowing where else to go, I wandered past a realtor's office and stepped into a recruiter's office. I had my nursing degree, they wanted and needed nurses on active duty. I signed up, they put me through some officer training and here I am." She held her arms out.

"Playing volleyball in Afghanistan, working on your tan during the day and helping soldiers at night." Rucker gave her a brief smile. "I, for one, appreciate what you're doing for our guys and gals."

"I do the best I can," she said softly. "I just wish I could do more. I'd rather stay here than redeploy back to the States, but they're afraid if they keep us here too long, we'll burn out or get PTSD."

"One week, huh?"

She nodded. "One week."

"In my field, one week to redeploy back to the States is a dangerous time. Anything can happen and usually does."

"Yeah, but you guys are on the frontlines, if not behind enemy lines. I'm back here. What could happen?"

Rucker flinched. "Oh, sweetheart, you didn't just say that..." He glanced around, hoping no one heard her tempt fate with those dreaded words *What could happen?*

Nora grinned. "You're not superstitious, are you?"

"In what we do, we can't afford not to be," he said, tossing salt over his shoulder.

"I'll be fine," she said in a reassuring, nurse's voice.

"Stop," he said, holding up his hand. "You're only digging the hole deeper." He tossed more salt over his other shoulder.

Nora laughed.

"Don't laugh." He handed her the saltshaker. "Do it."

"I'm not tossing salt over my shoulder. Someone has to clean the mess hall."

Rucker leaned close and shook salt over her shoulder. "I don't know if it counts if someone else throws salt over your shoulder, but I figure you now need every bit of luck you can get."

"You're a fighter but afraid of a little bad luck." Nora shook her head. "Those two things don't seem to go together."

"You'd be surprised how easily my guys are freaked by the littlest things."

"And you," she reminded him.

"You asking *what could happen?* isn't a little thing. That's in-your-face tempting fate." Rucker was laying it on thick to keep her grinning, but deep down, he believed what he was saying. And it didn't make a difference the amount of education he had or the statistics that predicted outcomes. His gut told him she'd just tempted fate with her statement. Maybe he was overthinking things. Now, he was worried she wouldn't make it back to the States alive.

* * *

Nora liked Rucker. He was the first guy who'd walked away without an argument since she'd arrived at the base in Afghanistan. He'd meant what he'd said and proved it. His dark brown hair and deep green eyes, coupled with broad shoulders and a narrow waist, made him even more attractive. Not all the men were in as good a shape as Rucker. And he seemed to have a very determined attitude.

She hadn't known what to expect when she'd deployed. Being the center of attention of almost every single male on the base hadn't been one of her expectations. She'd only ever considered herself average in the looks department. But when the men outnumbered women by more than ten to one, she guessed average appearance moved up in the ranks.

"Where did you learn to play volleyball?" Rucker asked, changing the subject of her leaving and her flippant comment about what could happen in one week.

"I was on the volleyball team in high school. It got me a scholarship to a small university in my home state of Minnesota, where I got my Bachelor of Science degree in Nursing."

"It takes someone special to be a nurse," he stated. "Is that what you always wanted to be?"

She shook her head. "I wanted to be a firefighter when I was in high school."

"What made you change your mind?"

She stared down at the coffee growing cold in her mug. "My mother was diagnosed with cancer when I was a senior in high school. I wanted to help but felt like I didn't know enough to be of assistance." She looked up. "She made it through chemo and radiation treatments and still came to all of my volleyball games. I thought she was in the clear."

"She wasn't?" Rucker asked, his tone low and gentle.

"She didn't tell me any different. When I got the scholarship, I told her I wanted to stay close to home to be with her. She insisted I go and play volleyball for the university. I was pretty good and played for the first two years I was there. I quit the team in my third year to start the nursing program. I didn't know there was anything wrong back home. I called every week to talk to Mom. She never let on that she was sick." She forced a smile. "But you don't want my sob story. You probably want to know what's going on around here."

He set his mug on the table. "If we were alone in a coffee bar back in the States, I'd reach across the table and take your hand."

"Oh, please. Don't do that." She looked around the mess hall, half expecting someone might have over- heard Rucker's comment. "You're enlisted. I'm an officer. That would get us into a whole lot of trouble."

"Yeah, but we're also two human beings. I wouldn't be human if I didn't feel empathy for you and want to provide comfort."

She set her coffee cup on the table and laid her hands in her lap. "I'll be satisfied with the thought. Thank you."

"Doesn't seem like enough. When did you find out your mother was sick?"

She swallowed the sadness that welled in her throat every time she remembered coming home to find out her mother had been keeping her illness from her. "It wasn't until I went home for Christmas in my senior year that I realized she'd been lying to me for a while." She laughed in lieu of sobbing. "I don't care who they are, old people don't always tell the truth."

"How long had she been keeping her sickness from you?"

"She'd known the cancer had returned halfway through my junior year. I hadn't gone home that summer because I'd been working hard to get my coursework and clinical hours in the nursing program. When I went home at Christmas..." Nora gulped. "She wasn't the same person. She'd lost so much weight and looked twenty years older."

"Did you stay home that last semester?" Rucker asked.

"Mom insisted I go back to school and finish what

I'd started. Like your mother, she hadn't gone to college. She wanted her only child to graduate. She was afraid that if I stayed home to take care of her, I wouldn't finish my nursing degree."

"I heard from a buddy of mine that those programs can be hard to get into," he said. "I can see why she wouldn't want you to drop everything in your life to take care of her."

Nora gave him a watery smile. "That's what she said. As soon as my last final was over, I returned to my hometown. I became her nurse. She lasted another three months before she slipped away."

"That's when you joined the Army?"

She shook her head. "Dad was so heartbroken, I stayed a few months until he was feeling better. I got a job at a local emergency room. On weekends, my father and I worked on cleaning out the house and getting it ready to put on the market."

"Is your dad still alive?" Rucker asked.

Nora nodded. "He lives in Texas. He moved to a small house with a big backyard." She forced a smile. "He has a garden, and all the ladies in his retirement community think he's the cat's meow. He still misses Mom, but he's getting on with his life."

Rucker tilted his head. "When did you join the military?"

"When Dad sold the house and moved into his retirement community. I worried about him, but he's doing better."

"And you?"

"I miss her. But she'd whip my ass if I wallowed in self-pity for more than a moment. She was a strong woman and expected me to be the same."

Rucker grinned. "From what I've seen, you are."

Nora gave him a skeptical look. "You've only seen me playing volleyball. It's just a game." Not that she'd admit it, but she was a real softy when it came to caring for the sick and injured.

"If you're half as good at nursing, which I'm willing to bet you are, you're amazing." He started to reach across the table for her hand. Before he actually touched her, he grabbed the saltshaker and shook it over his cold breakfast.

"You just got in this morning?" Nora asked.

Rucker nodded.

"How long will you be here?" she asked.

"I don't know."

"What do you mean, you don't know? I thought when people were deployed, they were given a specific timeframe."

"Most people are. We're deployed where and when needed."

Nora frowned. "What are you? Some kind of special forces team?"

His lips pressed together. "Can't say."

She sat back. He was some kind of Special Forces. "Army, right?"

He nodded.

That would make him Delta Force. The elite of the elite. A very skilled soldier who undertook incredibly dangerous missions. She gulped and stopped herself from reaching across the table to take his hand. "Well, I hope all goes well while you and your team are here."

"Thanks."

A man hurried across the chow hall wearing shorts and an Army T-shirt. He headed directly toward their table.

Nora didn't recognize him. "Expecting someone?" she asked Rucker, tipping her head toward the man.

Rucker turned, a frown pulling his eyebrows together. "Why the hell's Dash awake?"

Nora frowned. "Dash? Please tell me that's his callsign, not his real name."

Rucker laughed. "It should be his real name. He's first into the fight, and he's fast." Rucker stood and faced his teammate. "What's up?"

"CO wants us all in the Tactical Operations Center," Dash said. "On the double."

"Guess that's my cue to exit." Rucker turned to Nora. "I enjoyed our talk."

She nodded. "Me, too."

Dash grinned. "Tell you what...I'll stay and finish your conversation while you see what the commander wants."

Rucker hooked Dash's arm twisted it up behind his back, and gave him a shove toward the door. "You heard the CO, he wants all of us." Rucker winked at Nora. "I hope to see you on the volleyball court before you leave."

"Same. Good luck." Nora's gaze followed Rucker's broad shoulders and tight ass out of the chow hall. Too bad she'd only be there another week before she shipped out. She would've enjoyed more volleyball and coffee with the Delta Force operative.

He'd probably be on maneuvers that entire week.

She stacked her tray and coffee cup in the collection area and left the chow hall, heading for the building where she shared her quarters with Beth Drennan, a nurse she'd become friends with during their deployment together.

As close as they were, Nora didn't bring up her conversation with the Delta. With only a week left at the base, she probably wouldn't run into him again. Though she would like to see him again, she prayed he didn't end up in the hospital.

# ABOUT THE AUTHOR

ELLE JAMES also writing as MYLA JACKSON is a *New York Times* and *USA Today* Bestselling author of books including cowboys, intrigues and paranormal adventures that keep her readers on the edges of their seats. When she's not at her computer, she's traveling, snow skiing, boating, or riding her ATV, dreaming up new stories. Learn more about Elle James at www.ellejames.com

Website | Facebook | Twitter | GoodReads | Newsletter | BookBub | Amazon

Or visit her alter ego Myla Jackson at mylajackson.com
Website | Facebook | Twitter | Newsletter

*Follow Me!*
www.ellejames.com
ellejamesauthor@gmail.com

# ALSO BY ELLE JAMES

Shadow Assassin

***Delta Force Strong***

Ivy's Delta (Delta Force 3 Crossover)

Breaking Silence (#1)

Breaking Rules (#2)

Breaking Away (#3)

Breaking Free (#4)

Breaking Hearts (#5)

Breaking Ties (#6)

Breaking Point (#7)

Breaking Dawn (#8)

Breaking Promises (#9)

***Brotherhood Protectors Yellowstone***

Saving Kyla (#1)

Saving Chelsea (#2)

Saving Amanda (#3)

Saving Liliana (#4)

Saving Breely (#5)

Saving Savvie (#6)

Saving Jenna (#7)

Drake (#6)

Grimm (#7)

Murdock (#8)

Utah (#9)

Judge (#10)

### The Outriders

Homicide at Whiskey Gulch (#1)

Hideout at Whiskey Gulch (#2)

Held Hostage at Whiskey Gulch (#3)

Setup at Whiskey Gulch (#4)

Missing Witness at Whiskey Gulch (#5)

Cowboy Justice at Whiskey Gulch (#6)

### Hellfire Series

Hellfire, Texas (#1)

Justice Burning (#2)

Smoldering Desire (#3)

Hellfire in High Heels (#4)

Playing With Fire (#5)

Up in Flames (#6)

Total Meltdown (#7)

### Declan's Defenders

Marine Force Recon (#1)

Show of Force (#2)

Full Force (#3)

Driving Force (#4)

Tactical Force (#5)

Disruptive Force (#6)

### Mission: Six

One Intrepid SEAL

Two Dauntless Hearts

Three Courageous Words

Four Relentless Days

Five Ways to Surrender

Six Minutes to Midnight

### Hearts & Heroes Series

Wyatt's War (#1)

Mack's Witness (#2)

Ronin's Return (#3)

Sam's Surrender (#4)

### Take No Prisoners Series

SEAL's Honor (#1)

SEAL'S Desire (#2)

SEAL's Embrace (#3)

SEAL's Obsession (#4)

SEAL's Proposal (#5)

SEAL's Seduction (#6)

Hot Velocity (#4)

**Cajun Magic Mystery Series**

Voodoo on the Bayou (#1)

Voodoo for Two (#2)

Deja Voodoo (#3)

Cajun Magic Mysteries Books 1-3

**SEAL Of My Own**

Navy SEAL Survival

Navy SEAL Captive

Navy SEAL To Die For

Navy SEAL Six Pack

**Devil's Shroud Series**

Deadly Reckoning (#1)

Deadly Engagement (#2)

Deadly Liaisons (#3)

Deadly Allure (#4)

Deadly Obsession (#5)

Deadly Fall (#6)

**Covert Cowboys Inc Series**

Triggered (#1)

Taking Aim (#2)

Bodyguard Under Fire (#3)

***Boys Behaving Badly Anthologies***

Rogues (#1)

Blue Collar (#2)

Pirates (#3)

Stranded (#4)

First Responder (#5)

Blown Away

Warrior's Conquest

Enslaved by the Viking Short Story

Conquests

Smokin' Hot Firemen

Protecting the Colton Bride

Protecting the Colton Bride & Colton's Cowboy Code

Heir to Murder

Secret Service Rescue

High Octane Heroes

Haunted

Engaged with the Boss

Cowboy Brigade

Time Raiders: The Whisper

Bundle of Trouble

Killer Body

Operation XOXO

An Unexpected Clue